7 MINUTES IN HEAVEN

ARE YOU GAME?

RHIAN CAHILL

RHIAN CAHILL

7 Minutes In Heaven
Are You Game? Book 1
By Rhian Cahill

Copyright © 2018 Rhian Cahill
ISBN: 978-1-925375-12-1
Cover by Valerie Tibbs of Tibbs Design

All rights reserved. No part of this book may be reproduced, scanned, or distributed in any printed or electronic form without permission. Please do not participate in or encourage piracy of copyrighted materials in violation of the author's rights.

This is a work of fiction. Names, places, characters and incidents are the product of the author's imagination and are fictitious. Any resemblance to actual persons, living or dead, events or establishments is solely coincidental.

For more information visit:
www.rhiancahill.com

DEDICATION

For all those afraid of the dark, it doesn't always hide monsters.
For the man I'd gladly get in the closet with. Mr.C, you don't need seven minutes to rock my world, you do it every second you love me.

1

Cassie clamped her jaw and clenched her fists. She would not rise to the Neanderthal in front of her. Lil had been gone only an hour and already this giant was throwing his weight around. Lillian McDermott may be her best friend and done Cassie a huge favor when she agreed to be the first to host the new line of adult parties run by Are You Game?, but that didn't mean Cassie, or her team, could be anything except professional. This was still a job.

A job that could break her company's good reputation or send it skyrocketing. She'd do anything to continue the success of Are You Game?, and if it meant putting up with the head of McDermott Security—aka Mr. Muscles—then Cassie would suck it up and deal.

Taking a deep breath, she focused her mind on her job—on making Lillian McDermott's farewell bash the party of the year. Calmer, Cassie tilted her head up and met eyes as black as coal and just as cold. It made her pause, the darkness lurking in that piercing gaze. He stood almost a foot taller than her, and if she were a simpering female, she might actually be afraid of the menacing giant. But Cassandra Moreland had never been simpering or particularly female. Growing up with five older brothers had fixed that.

She drew in another deep breath and let it out slowly. "Look. I know Lil left you and your team to oversee the rest of the night, but it's me and my team that are in charge of this event and the cleanup. I'd appreciate it if you and your men stay out of our way."

"Cassie."

Her eyes narrowed. Oh, how she hated that placating tone men used when they were trying to reason with a *difficult* woman. "Don't take that tone with me." She stepped closer.

His eyes flashed. Fire lit up the dark depths for a split second before he blinked and cut the emotion—if that's what is was—off. Not one to back down, Cassie pushed to her toes and got as close to in his face as she could without getting a stepladder. Her chest brushed his and the zing that shot through her system couldn't be mistaken for anything but desire. Cassie's breath stalled in her lungs and whatever words she'd been about to blast him with died on her tongue.

Holy shit!

She sank back to her heels, but before they touched the floor, he shot out his hands and grabbed her elbows.

"Oh no, don't back down now, Cass." He used his grip to pull her back against him. "Not when things are just getting interesting."

They eyed each other for long moments, and Cassie had the impression he was sizing her up—testing her mettle—before making another move. She wasn't sure what to do or think. For a start, he was manhandling her. That hadn't happened since she was in the eighth grade and Malcolm Birmingham had gotten a little too fresh on their first date. But unlike then, she didn't bring her knee up to rearrange the giant's groin. No, she wanted to reach down and cup it.

Oh boy.

He leaned closer, his lips a breath from hers. "Do you really want me to stay out of your way?"

Oh God.

Cassie's mouth went dry. The man held her spellbound, and she didn't even know his name. She darted her tongue out to wet her lips, except he was so close the tip slid over his full bottom lip before retreating into her mouth. They both sucked in a sharp breath and Cassie's eyes widened, her heart thudding as his dark gaze bore into hers. His nostrils flared and air streamed across her face as he inhaled and exhaled in a gusty breath.

He smelled of peppermint, and she was reminded of when she was little and her grandma would sneak her chewing gum when her parents weren't looking. It made her feel safe—loved—and didn't that just blow her mind.

"Cassie?" Her head snapped around to find Dan standing beside them. "Everything okay?"

"Um…" She had no clue what to tell her second-in-charge.

"No problem," the giant said as he lowered her feet to the floor and set her away from him. "We were just trying to hear each other without yelling."

Cassie's eyes met those breath-stealing dark orbs once more and a frisson of heat arrowed through her belly. "Ah, yeah, um, just sorting out the remainder of the evening."

"Right, well we're out of scotch, vodka *and* tequila. Oh, and the last of the finger food is being circulated as we speak," Dan said.

"We're out of food?" she asked, turning her attention back to Dan.

"Not quite yet." Dan watched a waiter pass by, the silver tray he carried half-empty. "But it won't be long."

"That's okay. We're winding things down anyway." Cassie turned back to face Mr. Muscles. "We'll start shutting down the bars."

He crossed his arms over his massive chest and Cassie tried really hard not to ogle the mouth-watering pecs hidden beneath his tight black shirt. When she brought her gaze up to meet his, it was to find one dark brow arched and a look on his face that clearly said he was pleased he'd gotten his way.

Damn the man. She hated to give an inch to anyone, and if it weren't for the prospect of being in the house with no food or alcohol and a bunch of demanding partiers, she'd never bow to his demands to shut the party down and usher everyone out. The plan had been to allow the evening to come to a natural end, only now it appeared as though he'd be getting his way.

With no small amount of frustration and anger, Cassie added, "We'll start cleanup, you and your men stay out of our way." She spun on her heel and, spine and shoulders straight, marched off, praying no one could see her shaking. The giant specimen of seething testosterone set her on edge, the least of which was the blade of arousal she felt for a man whose name she didn't know.

LUCAS WILHELM WATCHED Cassandra Moreland walk away. The word 'run' slid through his mind, but Cassie wasn't the type of woman to run from anything—or anyone. Hell, if he didn't know better he'd think she actually had a set of balls in those sexy black pants of hers.

A smile tugged at his mouth and it took more than the usual effort to keep his face impassive. He was going to enjoy tangling with little Miss In Charge. Surveying the crowd, Luc doubted she'd be getting anyone out of here anytime soon. Not without pulling the fire alarm and starting the sprinkler system. Eyeing the couple in the far corner, he wondered if a drenching wasn't exactly what this party needed.

There were sweaty half-naked bodies all over the house. All gyrating to the pounding beat of the music thumping through the wireless speakers in a very adult bump and grind that was more sex than dance. Luc shook his head and moved through the room toward the front of the house. He spotted two of his men and motioned them over to give them orders.

"Where do you want us, boss?"

"I need the backyard and deck cleared. Herd everyone into the house and close the doors behind them." If they could slowly push everyone out the front door it would help Cassie, not that he expected her to be happy with him lending a hand. His lips curled. He looked forward to the argument they would surely have in the next little while. "And when you're done out there, start moving everyone into the front rooms."

"On it, Mr. Wilhelm."

Luc hated it when his men called him Mr. Wilhelm. It always gave him the urge to look over his shoulder for his father. Stifling the action, he nodded at the two men and continued through to the front door. Two more of his men stood either side of the wide-open double doors as though they were sentries stopping anyone from escaping, except he *wanted* the guests to get away.

"You two, upstairs. Start clearing out all the rooms. And check the closets." Lord knows what games people were playing up there. So far he'd seen more than one he'd played himself back when getting a hot piece of ass was all he was about. Of course, those days were long gone. In fact, he couldn't remember the last time he'd wanted to get his hands on any ass. Well, not before one pint-sized brunette went toe-to-toe with him, anyway.

Another smile tugged at his lips, and Luc marveled at the emotion one small woman could drag out of him when men twice her size couldn't make him so much as twitch.

He glanced at his watch. Two minutes after two. Time to put party shutdown into overdrive. Stalking through the downstairs rooms, Luc found each of his men and sent them out to move the crowd along. It was similar to herding sheep. En masse, they surged into the front of the house, filling the areas to breathing room only.

In twos and threes, sometimes more, they began to disappear out the front door and into the night. By the time Lachlan McDermott barreled into the living room, steam shooting from his ears, the place was down to half the number of occupants there had been when Luc first arrived.

The boss wasn't happy. And the silence that filled the house when Lachlan yanked out the DJ's power cables hurt Luc's ears. He swiftly made his way over to the man who personally signed his paycheck.

"Where's Lucas?" Lachlan growled at one of McDermott Security's men.

"Right behind you, boss," Luc answered.

Lachlan spun around. "Where's Mac?"

"He took Ms. McDermott off site about an hour ago. Maybe

more." Luc steeled himself. He had no doubt Lachlan wouldn't be happy with Mackenzie and Lillian's whereabouts.

"Off site? During a party Lil is responsible for?"

Luc nodded and kept his expression bland. He didn't want to give Lachlan McDermott any reason to stop signing those checks. "Mr. Harris arranged for my team to take charge. I've been monitoring the situation."

Numerous emotions flashed across Lachlan's face while he glanced around the room. Bringing his gaze back to Luc he said, "Get 'em out. All of them."

Inclining his head once more, Luc gave the only reply he could. "Consider it done, boss."

The fact Lachlan turned and strode from the room without a backward glance told Luc that not only was his pay safe but he was trusted to do the job given him. Breathing a little easier, he turned to the man on his right. "You heard the boss. Get 'em out."

His employee spun into action and Luc went in search of Cassie. She would not be pleased when he informed her they were shutting down effective immediately. He'd be a liar if he said the swirling in his gut wasn't excitement. But going toe-to-toe with Cassandra Moreland had more than his stomach churning. The tightness in his pants hadn't escaped his notice either.

And wasn't that an interesting development. He didn't usually go for bossy, confrontational females. Or ones that didn't even come up to his chin. Luc scrubbed a hand over his stubbled jaw. This evening was turning out to be far more entertaining than he'd ever expected.

CASSIE WAS LOADING empty bottles into a recycling bag when someone grabbed her arm and propelled her across the kitchen, forcing her to jog or fall on her face. "Hey!"

"We need to talk."

Great. Mr. Muscles was manhandling her again. Yanking on her arm proved ineffective in gaining freedom from his vise-like grip, so she swung her full weight to the left and slammed into his rock-hard chest. Air burst from her lungs. *Holy shit.* The man was made of steel. Her brain rattled and any protest she might have uttered vibrated right off the thought train and into the fog this man's presence seemed to bring.

Dammit. She was a highly intelligent woman who ran her own business. Why the hell couldn't she think of anything other than exploring the slab of muscle she was currently plastered to? And it wasn't just her hands itching to wander new territory either.

Before she could ponder that thought any further he'd maneuvered them into the walk-in pantry and closed the door. For a heartbeat, the room remained pitch black, then he bumped his shoulder against the wall and eye-straining fluorescent brilliance flooded the area. His hands spanned her waist and it took her a second to realize he'd carried her the last few steps and still held her off the floor. She was eye level with his mouth.

The very mouth she'd inadvertently caught a taste of earlier. The one she wanted to take a bigger sample of now.

Cassie swallowed, her throat dry, and fought the urge to lean in to seize the kiss she craved. She moved her gaze up his slightly crooked nose and met those dark, dark eyes. Her heart kicked. How had she ever thought his eyes were cold? Heat turned the brown—not black as she'd previously thought—irises into molten pools of hunger that flared hotter as their gazes connected. She gasped. The beat of her heart stepped up double-time and she went soft in places she hadn't thought about in a long time. Who *was* this man and what the fuck was he doing to her?

"W-who are you?" Her voice came out a timid whisper, but she couldn't summon the energy or desire to be offended by her sudden lack of backbone.

"You know who I am."

His deep voice rumbled in her ears and sent shockwaves of sensation skittering over her skin. A shiver slid down her spine as warmth flickered into flame in her belly. She licked her lips. "No. No, I don't."

"Cass," he whispered as he moved closer. "I'm the man who's going to bring you to your knees."

Oh God.

He brushed her lips with his, the move slow and steady, allowing plenty of time for her to turn away. Only she didn't. Instead, she moved into him. Met him halfway and took as much as she gave.

They didn't ease into the kiss—they dove deep. He thrust his tongue against hers, caressed and teased until she was panting for breath and thinking they had way too many clothes on.

Cassie tilted her head and moaned when he took advantage of the better angle. The kiss went on and on. Each slide, each lick, each nip, drove her further into the sexual haze surrounding them.

He dug his fingers into her waist as he tightened his grip and crushed her against him. Her breasts pressed into solid muscle, her nipples going taut on contact with the hot wall of his chest. She tore her mouth from his and gasped for breath only to lose any hope of breathing normally when he trailed his lips over her chin and down her neck. He sucked and nibbled, devouring every centimeter of skin left bare above her collar. Every nerve ending buzzed until her blood hummed with the all-consuming lust flooding her system.

Cassie tangled her fingers in his hair, the silky strands curling around them as though tying her to him. She didn't remember wrapping her arms around him. Didn't remember hooking her legs around his waist either, but she couldn't deny she was currently covering him like shrink-wrap. He bucked his hips and his very impressive erection pressed into her sex.

There was no stopping her hips from thrusting back, from grinding her clit on the hard length of his cock in her search for relief. For more. With a growl, his mouth came back to hers and she lost herself in the sublime talent of his tongue.

He slid his hands up her sides, his thumbs coming to rest on the lower curve of her breasts, and another growl rumbled through his chest as she wiggled in an attempt to move his hands higher. He didn't disappoint.

With skill, he maneuvered those big hands between them and

cupped her full mounds in his palms. Her nipples throbbed and she arched her back, pressing her breasts deeper into his hold. She needed more. So much more. Cassie sucked his tongue into her mouth and then slowly let it out, raking her teeth along the sides as she did. The pounding of her heart echoed in her ears and through her body, thumping with a bone-jarring intensity.

He tore his mouth from hers and growled, "Fuck."

She couldn't catch her breath, couldn't fathom the change when he tried to push her away. "What?"

His dark gaze met hers, his chest heaving as he dragged in air. "There's someone banging on the door."

"What?"

He lowered his forehead to rest it on hers. "There's someone knocking on the door behind me."

Cassie's lust-fogged brain took another second to comprehend the meaning of his words, but when it did mortification swamped her. She was in a client's pantry making out with a guy she didn't know. With a groan, she closed her eyes and dropped her head to the side, butting her brow against his shoulder.

How could she forget where she was and what she was supposed to be doing? And why the hell was she still wrapped around this stranger like a wet Speedo on a Bondi lifesaver? A shiver rolled over her.

Oh, *so* not the right analogy to be thinking. She should be concentrating on getting herself off. Another shiver rippled through her. Oh God, not *off* off. Cassie dropped her legs and tried to unravel her arms from the giant's neck. But her feet didn't touch the floor and his large hands on her waist held her prisoner against him. Her heart raced with residual arousal and the embarrassment of her recent behavior, while her mind spun in circles in search of what to say.

"Cass."

Damn. The man knew how to use his voice to make her sit up and take notice. She never knew her name could render her senseless with desire. Except the way he said it, in that deep, gravely tone, made her insides not only sit up but dance a little jig too. Cassie swallowed over the lump in her throat and blurted out the first words that came to mind.

"I don't even know your name." Heat scorched her face. She'd spent the last few minutes locked in a pantry making out with a stranger. It was the one game she hadn't put on tonight's list—not that it had stopped some of the guests from playing it.

7 Minutes in Heaven.

Only seven minutes was nowhere near long enough with the man who held her in his arms. And altogether too long for her peace of mind.

2

Luc relaxed the muscles in his arms and did the one thing he really didn't want to. He set Cassie on her feet. Whoever had been hammering on the door had stopped, but the damage was done. Regret was written all over her pretty face. Scrubbing a hand over his stubbled jaw, he drew in a deep breath and let it out slowly.

"Luc," he said

Cassie's gaze met his, one delicate eyebrow arched.

"My name. It's Lucas Wilhelm. I'm head of McDermott Security, a position I've held for ten years." Luc added the last part in the hope of reassuring her.

"Oh. Um, well..." She lowered her eyes, hiding the uncertainty swirling in their honey-colored depths.

Placing two fingers under her chin, he tipped her head back until her gaze met his once more. "Don't back down now, Cass. Where's the woman who's fought me for control for the last couple of hours gone?"

She shook her head, dislodging his fingers. "She just had common sense kissed right out of her."

The small smile tugging at the corner of her mouth pulled at his gut and eased his mind. He hadn't been sure at first, but now he didn't doubt she'd bounce back from their mind-numbing lip-lock. Luc had expected they'd be explosive, he just hadn't realized how unstable their chemistry was. He'd have to keep his hands off her until they were in more suitable surroundings or they'd find themselves sans clothes. There was one sure-fire way to keep her at a distance though. Strip her of control.

"As of now, this party is over."

"What?" Her eyes narrowed to slits.

If looks could kill, the one she aimed his way would slice him to ribbons, and Luc figured she'd used it to de-ball many a man before him. Good thing he'd spent years developing a tough exterior. Although she'd found a way under his skin already, he wasn't about to cower before her hostile stare. Luc embraced the hum in his veins. The zap delivered courtesy of her returning ballsy attitude. He'd never gone looking for a fight. Sure he'd been in plenty, but he'd never started one. Except now. With Cassie. And there was no denying the thrill thrumming in his blood. He was more than looking forward to their combat. He was eager for it to begin.

"As you can hear, there's no longer music blasting through the house and that's thanks to Lachlan McDermott ripping out power cables. If I were you, I wouldn't be surprised when your DJ files a damage report and insurance claim." Luc smiled as a growl rumbled in her throat. He'd never heard that particular sound from a woman, and he'd certainly never found it a turn on coming from any man, but there was no mistaking the tightening of his sac or the hardening of his cock.

"Damn men." Cassie shoved past him and flung open the door, using it to push him out of the way.

Before he got his head in gear and made it out from behind the door, she'd disappeared into the kitchen. With long strides, Luc followed only to witness her sexy ass vanish through the far doorway. Covering the distance in seconds, he found his men doing as he'd ordered. Between them and Cassie's staff, the guests were quickly being ushered from the house in a tidal wave of drunkenness.

His search for Cassie was hindered by the surge of bodies moving toward the front door. With his chances to spot her zero he let himself be swept up in the tide. When he reached the front yard, hire cars and drivers lined the street. Inebriated partiers tumbled into backseats, car doors slammed and departing vehicles were quickly swallowed up by the night.

With the party down to the last few stragglers, he turned back to the house determined to find Cassie while his men dealt with the remaining guests. He found her back in the kitchen. Leaning his shoulder against the doorframe, he folded his arms, crossed one ankle over the other and watched as she gave orders while packing box after box with glasses.

The image of efficiency, her movements were economical and fluid, her speed and accuracy proving she'd done this a thousand times before. Luc relaxed and enjoyed the view. His pants grew snug and he had to shift his stance to alleviate the pressure on his hardening cock.

She turned and stared straight at him. Her gaze traveled from his face to his toes and back again, the slow survey like a physical caress, and a shaft of heat speared his groin. A knowing smile graced her mouth and more fire exploded in his crotch as he remembered the taste of those lips. He pushed off the wall and angled his body so the evidence of his arousal wouldn't be so blatant. Cassie's gaze dipped and her smile grew, sending the heat in his groin licking along his veins until he burned from top to bottom—inside out.

The woman was dangerous, she poked at every nerve he had and flayed them raw without trying. Luc couldn't wait to have her beneath him.

"Are you going to stand there all night scaring my employees or are you planning to make yourself useful?"

Luc jerked at her words. He'd thought for sure she'd continue to ignore him, and he smiled as he stepped toward her. Her next words stopped him in his tracks.

"Oh wait, that's right, you don't take orders. You *give* them."

His gaze narrowed, the burst of anger he felt a total overreaction, but then every emotion involving Cassandra Moreland was exaggerated. The smart-aleck grin on her face didn't help either. Nor the fact she was just as averse to taking orders as he was. It wasn't as though he couldn't take them. It was more that he normally delivered them. He could take direction just as well as the next guy. He'd taken an order from Lachlan McDermott, hadn't he? And Cassie definitely couldn't talk. She was exactly the same if their recent interaction was anything to go by.

"Pot, meet Kettle," Luc mumbled.

Her shoulders straightened. "What did you call me?"

"You heard." He walked closer. "We're two peas in a pod, Cass, and you know it."

"Bullshit." She slammed the plastic lid on the tub in front of her and snapped the locking handles into place with unnecessary force. "I can take orders."

"Really?" Luc leaned on the bench that separated them. "Prove it."

Cassie's eyes widened before they reduced to narrow slits and his insides clenched. God, why did her anger get him off? And why the hell did he continue to poke at her? The suddenness of her smile didn't bode well, but Luc waited with bated breath for her next words. She didn't disappoint him.

"On one condition."

"What?"

"You do the same."

Oh, this was going to be good. Inwardly he smiled, but he didn't let any of his excitement at her obvious capitulation to his challenge show. "Deal."

"Wait, we haven't worked out the terms."

"That's the easy part. We'll each take orders from the other for twenty-four hours." Luc couldn't help it, he upped the ante. Leaning forward, he brought his face inches from hers. His gaze dropped to her lips and he watched as her tongue slipped out to slide along the plump pink flesh he wanted to taste again so badly he ached with it. "For a whole day, anything I tell you to do, you do and vice versa."

CASSIE SUCKED IN A BREATH. He couldn't be suggesting what she thought. "You don't mean..."

"Yeah, that's exactly what I mean."

She glanced around to make sure no one was listening. "You can't expect me to agree to this. You're basically propositioning me."

Lucas laughed. "Nice to know where your mind is, but I don't recall mentioning sex."

Damn. He was right, he hadn't mentioned sex, but he'd definitely implied it, what with the way he kept looking at her. Or was it because her mind had been on a continuous loop of imagined pleasure with Lucas ever since their kiss in the pantry? Fantasies of being naked with him had plagued her from the moment she'd walked away.

She couldn't help it, they might not have done much more than kiss, but her body had shot straight to overheated and stayed there. Her recent lack of a sex-life might have something to do with her fixation with the sexily muscled giant in front of her too. God, she couldn't remember the last time she'd had a man-delivered orgasm, and he'd promised to deliver one with only his lips.

Cassie took a calming breath—or at least she hoped the lungful of oxygen would be—and let her mind clear of carnal thoughts so she could at least weigh the pros and cons of being what effectively was this man's slave for twenty-four hours. If he had no intention of moving their little challenge into the bedroom then she could deal with any order he gave.

At least she thought she could. Hopefully he wouldn't get her to clean his bathroom. She didn't do boys' toilets anymore. She'd spent her teenage years sharing one bathroom with five brothers and not one of them had ever cleaned up after themselves.

Or aimed straight.

She studied the man on the other side of the counter. If he wasn't planning to take this arrangement into the sexual arena then what was his agenda? Could she trust him to keep his word if she agreed?

"What's wrong, Cass? You afraid you can't handle me telling you what to do?"

Hah! "I can handle anything you dish out. Question is, can you say the same?"

Cassie hoped he couldn't see through her tough-girl act, because in spite of a lifetime spent being scared of nothing, this man had her insides shaking and her nerves jittering with a healthy dose of fear.

It wasn't the thought of taking orders that had her worried either. Her brothers had bossed her around for as long as she could remember, so she knew she was capable of putting up with Lucas telling her what to do. She was more concerned about her traitorous libido.

The electricity arcing between them was enough to light up the entire city of Sydney for a month. But she'd be damned if she'd let him get the better of her.

He chuckled. "No question. It would take more than some little woman to scare me."

A growl rumbled in her chest. "Did you just call me a *little woman*?"

Lucas shrugged. "If the shoe fits."

Oh boy. That did it. She'd spent her whole life proving her size didn't matter. She might be average height for a female, but in a household of extra-tall individuals that hadn't made a difference. As the shortest, she'd endured every tease imaginable from her brothers, and hearing Lucas refer to her as 'little' only tweaked her need to prove she packed as big of a punch as he did.

"Fine." She stuck out her hand. "When do you want to start?"

"Now's as good a time as any." His large hand engulfed hers.

"I'm in charge first."

He arched an eyebrow.

"I've got a job tomorrow, and Dan was going to help me but now you will."

His other eyebrow joined the first, his eyes widening. "A party?" he asked as he glanced around them.

"Don't worry. It's not an adults-only one." Cassie smiled. "I'm sure you'll be fine. It's a birthday party."

"Oh." Relief filled his face as he smiled.

Cassie had to hold back her laughter. She wasn't about to inform him he'd be spending six hours with a bunch of pink-tutu-wearing five-year-olds helping them make jewelry from tiny glass beads. "I'll give you my work address and you can meet me there in the morning to help me load up the supplies."

"I thought we were starting now."

"Oh, but I thought…" What had she thought? Cassie had just assumed they'd start in the morning; they were both still working after all.

"Okay, how about this." Lucas glanced at his watch. "We start the clock ticking when we finish up here. You get me for twenty-four hours, then I get you for twenty-four."

He held her with a look that sent shivers down her spine. "But when I finish here I'm going home to catch a couple of hours sleep before I have to prep for tomorrow's party."

"So will I." He grinned and Cassie's stomach fluttered. "You can get me to massage your feet before you hit the sack."

Cassie gulped. Good God, that wasn't all she'd like him to massage, and most of what she was thinking would be done *after* she hit the sack. "You're coming home with me?"

"Yep. Twenty-four hours is twenty-four hours." Lucas locked his gaze to hers, his stare and stance clearly telegraphing the words *I dare you to back out*.

She wasn't stupid by a long shot, but Cassie may have just made the dumbest deal of the century with a man who had already proven he could scramble her brain with a mere kiss.

LUC WATCHED myriad emotions flicker across Cassie's face before she straightened her spine and yanked her hand from his. How either of them had forgotten to let go before now was a mystery. Then again maybe not.

His hand felt cold without hers tucked inside it and the heat her touch generated still zipped up his arm and through his body, hitting every erogenous zone he had. He slipped his thumb through a belt loop and shoved his fingers into his front pocket, which only made the fit of his slacks tighter and his semi-hard cock even more uncomfortable. He removed his hand and placed it on the counter, palm down, and leaned forward. The urge to kiss her fired his nerve endings and scorched his veins with molten lust.

What was it about Cassandra Moreland that sparked such an incendiary reaction?

Luc couldn't recall any other woman having such an instant or profound effect on him. In fact, he couldn't remember the last woman to have any kind of effect on him other than annoyance. He'd never been one to make close connections with anyone. It came with the job.

Being head of security meant he had to be available twenty-four-seven, and the women he met in his line of work were usually the shallow money-grubbing kind of individual, and therefore even if he'd found his interest piqued by a woman she was unlikely to want anything to do with a lowly bodyguard.

Of course, there were the few who wanted to take a tumble between the sheets with a dangerous man, but they tended to have their curiosity satisfied fairly quickly.

He'd left one-night stands behind him sometime in his twenties. At thirty-eight he was extremely discriminatory about his choice of bed partner. He wasn't in it just to get his rocks off. That type of dalliance left him unsatisfied and more often than not feeling selfish, used and disgusted with himself and the woman he was with. Might explain why he couldn't remember the last woman he'd had sex with.

If he had his way that dry spell was about to be broken, but not this weekend. Luc wouldn't use their challenge to get Cassie into bed. No. When he slept with her it would be because they both wanted it with bone-deep need, not because either of them had ordered the other there.

And the quicker they got this place cleared out, the quicker he could work his magic and have her panting for him. He wasn't delusional though, he knew full well that he'd be panting just as hard and looked forward to one very long weekend of temptation and anticipation with Cassandra Moreland.

"I'll get a couple of my men to give you a hand with the pack up," he said.

"What?" Cassie turned from the clipboard she was marking items off on. "My staff is more than capable of doing their job."

Luc smiled. "I didn't say they couldn't—"

"Then don't imply it." She squared her shoulders as though preparing for a fight.

He held up his hands. "Whoa. All I'm doing is offering to help."

"Then offer, don't order." Her mouth stretched into a straight line, her lips pressed together, and Luc wanted to lean over and tease his tongue along the seam until she softened and the harsh lines were plump and wet.

"Fine." He pulled his thoughts out of his pants and tried a different track. "It's two-thirty a.m., give yourself and your staff a break by allowing me and my men to help you finish out the night. I'm sure everyone is more than ready to head home. You've been here since two this afternoon."

Cassie's eyes narrowed and she crossed her arms over her ample bosom, drawing his gaze. "Could you not ogle me while we're arguing? And how the hell do you know what time I got here? Have you been spying on me?"

Luc brought his gaze up to meet hers. "We're arguing?"

"That's all you heard?"

"Well, no, but it was certainly the part that got my attention. As for the other, no, you aren't being *spied on*, but the McDermotts' security is the highest priority and therefore anything pertaining to them I know about."

"Anything?" She arched a brow.

"Yes."

"So you know that Lil quit modeling?"

"Yes." Luc quickly surveyed the space around them and judged the area safe. He knew he wouldn't be telling Cassie anything Lillian

McDermott hadn't already divulged. "I also know all about her children's clothing label, Lilli Pond, and next month's launch of her signature fragrance, Golden Lilli."

"Oh."

"It's my job, Cass. I take it and the safety of those under my protection very seriously." He placed his hands on the counter and leaned closer. "Now, will you let me and my men help you? You can give us orders and I won't even count the time toward our little weekend challenge."

She chewed the corner of her bottom lip. Her white teeth worrying the flesh until it turned a deep red caused Luc's groin to tighten.

"Fine. I could use some help loading these boxes into the back of the van in the driveway."

Luc smiled as satisfaction slid through his belly. She might not like taking his help, but she wasn't stubborn enough to refuse it to prove a point. He just hoped the rest of their time together would run as smoothly.

3

Cassie lowered the box to the van floor and tried to ignore the ache in her back. She didn't normally cart around the heavy equipment, usually she left the serious lifting for Dan or one of the other guys, so she only had herself to blame for any injury she sustained. Lucas hadn't actually challenged her competency, but after their earlier conversation her life-long compulsion to prove herself had reared its ugly head and she'd been compelled to show him she was more than capable of doing the job.

Unfortunately, that meant a sore back, and unless she treated the area with a heat pack when she got home, she was bound to suffer for the next few days. Cursing her stubborn need to demonstrate she measured up in every way, Cassie straightened and winced as a sharp twinge of pain lanced her lumbar region.

With a groan, Cassie reached around and pressed her hands against her lower back. Arching slightly, she stretched the muscles and kneaded with her fingers. Two large hands covered hers, warm strong fingers working along her spine with harder pressure than her own. She slipped her hands free and allowed the far more skilled ones to take over.

The ache eased with each caress and she couldn't stop the small moans of relief the soothing massage roused. Cassie didn't have to turn around to know who was behind her. Lucas. Heat radiated off him, surrounding her with the aroma of soap and man and a tantalizing cologne she couldn't name.

She'd know his scent anywhere. Funny how so little time spent in his presence could engrave him so deeply on her memory banks. She closed her eyes and took a deep breath. The heat and smell of him soaked in, curled inside her and drew her nerves taut until Cassie thought she might snap at any moment. She dipped her head forward with a groan as he hit a particularly tight spot.

It didn't take him long to weed the knots out of her stiff muscles. Concentrating on Lucas and his magic hands, she didn't hear anyone approach until Dan spoke beside her.

"We're almost done, Cassie. Just the walkthrough and letting everyone go left to do."

Her eyes snapped open and a gust of air burst from her lungs. She jumped forward, almost toppling into the rear of the van in her effort to move away from Lucas. Righting herself, she turned to Dan and thanked the darkness surrounding them. She'd hate for him to see her flaming-red face.

"You can let everyone go now. I'll do the walkthrough and fix anything we've forgotten, but I doubt I'll find anything. You always do a brilliant job on clear-out."

"Are you sure?" Dan asked. "I can do the walkthrough with you."

"No, it's okay, I can manage. If you let everyone know they can leave I'll get started." Cassie stepped around both men then stopped abruptly. "Oh, and you can have tomorrow off. I've found someone else to help me, and you already pulled those extra shifts this week so you deserve to have a full weekend free."

"I didn't think anyone was available for Saturday this week," Dan said.

Cassie glanced at Lucas. "Um, well, no, but Lucas has agreed to give me a hand."

"He has?" Dan looked Lucas over from head to toe with a critical eye. "Does he know what type of party it is?"

Not wanting Dan to let the cat out of the bag, she grabbed his arm and led him toward where her staff waited and away from Lucas. Cassie quickly changed the topic and pointed Dan in a different direction. "Make sure everyone has a ride home when you let them go. A couple of the guys are new to the team and I'm not sure how they got here."

He waited until they were out of earshot before pulling from her grasp and turning on her. "What the fuck is going on, Cassie?"

She didn't want to get into it with Dan right now, so she gave him the bare minimum of information. "Nothing is going on. Lucas and I got to talking and he volunteered to give me hand sometime, and seeing how you really shouldn't have to do another shift this week, I thought tomorrow would be perfect."

Dan eyed her with suspicion, but she'd learnt long ago how to school her face. She wasn't the family poker champion for nothing.

"I know I'm missing something, but I'll take your word for it as long as you promise to ring me if anything fucks up."

Cassie smiled. Dan might sometimes behave like one of her overbearing brothers, but she could always rely on him to put business first. "Promise."

"I don't like it, but you're the boss."

"Honest, Dan, nothing is going on. Now go see to the staff and I'll catch you on Monday at the office. Don't forget we need to talk about bringing on another supervisor." Cassie gave his shoulder a little push in an attempt to nudge him into action.

Standing his ground, he studied her a minute longer before drawing in a big breath and letting it out in a rush. "Fine. See you Monday."

She watched Dan stride across the lawn to where everyone had gathered. Cassie knew he wasn't happy about her plans to bring in more staff. They'd argued about waiting to see how successful this new arm of the business was, but she could already tell the adult party theme would prove to be popular.

Besides, the children's party line had more than doubled in bookings over the last six months, so she'd already been contemplating employing a manager for that area. It would be nice to have a weekend free for once too. Movement beside her caught her eye, and she turned to find Lucas standing a few feet away.

He'd kept his distance while she'd been talking to Dan, but he quickly closed the gap when their eyes connected. He didn't say a word, just stared at her with that dark, penetrating gaze. It made her squirm, being under his scrutiny, and Cassie figured he'd spent years perfecting his silent treatment and using it to get his way.

Good thing she wasn't intimidated easily—also a good thing he had no clue as to how deeply he affected her. She had a feeling he wouldn't think twice about using any weakness he found to get what he wanted, and that included her traitorous libido. Shame she didn't have any idea what it was he was after.

A shiver stole down her spine as the summer breeze kicked up. At least she told herself it was the breeze that made her tremble. It wouldn't do to admit the man before her had her nerves vibrating with anticipation.

Breaking eye contact, Cassie turned toward the house and her final job of the night. She ignored the man at her heels. Ignored the heat emanating from his body. Ignored the enticing scent surrounding her. And would definitely ignore the burn of desire his presence delivered to every inch of her. Heading through the front door, Cassie cleared her mind of all smutty thoughts and began her walkthrough.

LUC FOLLOWED Cassie as she made her way through every room of the house. He was surprised at her thoroughness. Then again, after only a few hours he shouldn't have been. She'd never do a half-assed job on anything. Speaking of asses, the one in front of him was world class.

She wasn't one of those super-skinny chicks and she wasn't what would be called full-figured either. Sleekly muscled, the firm globes of her ass seesawed up and down as she walked. Each step drew his gaze and made his pulse pound until every inch of him throbbed with need. Her curves were just the right size to fit in his hands. The urge to feel her backside pressed up against his groin shuddered through him, and without thought, Luc stepped forward and crowded her into the small bathroom she was checking.

"What—"

"Shh." He pressed her against the vanity, but their height difference meant that perfect ass met his thighs. His rapidly hardening cock nudged her lower back and Luc ground his pelvis into her.

"Lucas." His name slipped passed her lips on a sharp breath.

Cassie's protest was weak. Especially when he could feel her push back against him, felt her wiggle her rear end as though trying to get closer. His gaze landed on the mirror in front of them and he focused on their reflection. Luc studied them.

He towered above her, his body curled over hers, and he watched her face as he lowered his head and brushed his lips over the shell of her ear. Her eyes closed and her tongue darted out. The pink tip slicked across her bottom lip and left an enticing trail of moisture.

A groan rumbled in his chest as the memory of kissing her swamped him. In a split second, he grabbed her hips, spun her around and lifted her to the counter top.

He didn't give her a chance to protest. Not that she did when his mouth landed on hers. Luc forgot finesse, forgot gentle.

With a savage thrust, he drove his tongue between her lips and took what he wanted. What he craved. She gave all she had. Her mouth ate at his with equal demand, and Luc could only think it wasn't enough. It would never be enough. They had to get naked. Now.

So much for his plan of not taking her to bed this weekend. Tearing his mouth from hers, he struggled to pull oxygen into his starving lungs.

"I want you," he panted.

"Yes." She tangled her fingers in his hair and tugged his mouth back to hers.

Luc let Cassie take control of the kiss. Let her take her fill while he worked out the best way to have her naked beneath him. A noise overhead startled him and the fog of lust clogging his mind cleared long enough that he remembered where they were. Whose house they were in.

Shit.

He pulled away and stepped back. Cassie tipped forward and he reached out to steady her.

"What?" Confusion swirled in her dilated eyes.

"Not here." Luc gripped her waist and lowered her to the floor.

He saw the second comprehension dawned. Her face flushed red and her gaze dropped from his, her shoulders hunching forward.

"Oh God," she whispered.

If he wasn't watching her so closely, he wouldn't have seen her mouth move, wouldn't have caught the edge of embarrassment in her words. With the tip of his index finger he pushed her chin up and waited for her eyes to meet his.

"Don't." Luc moved his hand to cradle her jaw. "You weren't the only one lost in here."

"But—"

He placed his thumb over her lips. "No buts. And don't for one second think I was any less involved in this. I want you, Cass, more than I should I'm sure. But when I have you it won't be in the bathroom of the man who signs my paychecks."

"Jesus. I can't believe I forgot where we are. *Again.*" She smiled. "Thank you for not leaving me out on a limb on my own. I appreciate your honesty."

Luc cupped her face in both hands and leaned forward until his lips brushed hers. "One thing you can count on from me is honesty. I'll never lie to you. Now, let's finish your walkthrough and get out of here."

Cassie took a deep breath. "Um...maybe you should wait for me outside."

He chuckled. "I think I can keep my hands off you long enough to make it through the last couple of rooms, but if you think you can't..."

She grinned at him before she ducked under his arm and darted out of the bathroom. "Meet you by the front door," she called over her shoulder as she disappeared into the library across the hall.

Figuring Cassie might be right and they could do with some distance, Luc took his time as he made his way to the front door. He still hadn't told her she was his ride home.

Not that he was going home. As soon as she finished here their deal would start. Luc sighed. That meant he shouldn't take her to bed. There was no way he wanted her to think the bet they'd shaken on had anything to do with the two of them getting naked. Except he couldn't seem to keep his hands off her, and once he got his hands on her...well, nothing but getting her naked mattered.

He'd never been so taken—so out of control—with a woman before, and he had to make sure she knew this wasn't his usual behavior. He didn't ravish women within hours of meeting them. He leaned against the wall next to the door and waited for Cassie to finish. Luc didn't have to wait long. She was walking toward him as he thumbed through a news feed on his phone when a grainy photo popped up on the screen and changed his plans for the rest of the night.

"Son-of-a-bitch!" he growled as he straightened off the wall.

"Lucas?" Cass stopped a few feet away. "Is everything all right?"

Damn. How to tell the woman he'd planned to bed that he had to take a rain check.

CASSIE WATCHED emotions flicker across Lucas's face. It was the most expressive she'd seen him. Well, except for those few minutes in the bathroom. Watching his face in the mirror had been eye opening.

The man was not the cold giant he'd first appeared. He was madly swiping his fingers across his phone and whatever it was he was seeing didn't make him happy.

"I have to make a few calls. Can you wait while I do?" he asked, not taking his eyes off his screen.

She shrugged. "Sure. But don't you have Bluetooth in your car?"

His gaze snapped up. "I don't have my car. Mr. Harris took it when he and Ms. McDermott left earlier."

"Oh, so how were you... Oh." Cassie wasn't sure how she felt about him catching a ride with her. It made sense, what with their deal and all, but still. She'd be stuck with him. Anyone else wouldn't cause her insides to churn. Or her breath to quicken. No. Only the thought of being trapped in her van with Lucas could make her knees shake and her heart pound.

The man was far more dangerous than he looked, and to the average Joe he looked deadly.

He'd gone back to staring at his phone, his scowl becoming more menacing by the second. Sensing his need for privacy, Cassie moved toward the open door, but he stopped her with a hand on her arm.

"Just give me a minute." He didn't look at her, just tapped away at his screen.

Cassie didn't know what to do. On the one hand, she wanted to leave and let him do whatever it was he needed to, and on the other, she wanted to go back to when she was his single focus instead of the piece of technology in his hand. She sighed.

How selfish was that? He obviously had a problem, and all she could think about was she no longer had his attention.

"I'll wait outside."

His gaze met hers. The eyes she'd once thought cold probed hers for long moments. He nodded. "I'll only be a few minutes."

"Okay."

She made her escape and sucked in a lungful of cool morning air. Cassie wasn't sure what would happen when he finally came outside. Whether they'd pick up where they left off in the bathroom or if they'd remain caught in the tension of moments ago. One thing she was certain of was that Lucas Wilhelm was the first man in months to kiss her and the only man to ever render her speechless doing so.

Cassie headed for the van. Disengaging the locks, she hopped up in the driver's seat and shut the door. Only the confines of the cab were too small and she shoved the door open again. While warm, the night wasn't stifling enough to warrant turning the engine on and cranking the AC. Mind you, if Lucas heard the motor turn over he might think she was leaving without him, and that was the last thing she planned to do.

Jittery with nerves, she jumped from the van and paced to the rear and back again. By the time Lucas came out of the house and walked toward her, she'd almost worn a trench in the driveway and made what felt like life-altering decisions.

"All set. Ready to go?" Lucas asked as he reached her side.

"Definitely." What scared Cassie was just how ready she was to take this man home with her.

4

Cassie hadn't said a word since they'd pulled away from the McDermott house, but Luc didn't have time to worry whether it was a bad sign or not. He was too busy emailing and texting with his staff and the head of McDermott's PR division.

In the last thirty minutes, they'd managed to do nothing to stop the photos of Lachlan McDermott and Cameron Winters making out in a public park from hitting the news and every social media network on the planet. Luc would love to get his hands on Carl Holston for one minute. That's all it would take him to teach the scumbag photographer a lesson.

When the van finally stopped, Luc looked up. He'd barely taken notice of where they were going while Cassie drove, and it pained him to admit that if he hadn't known where Are You Game? was located he wouldn't have a clue where in Sydney they were. So much for his highly tuned observation skills.

He glanced around to discover they weren't at Cassie's work but in the driveway of a neat brick house with well-maintained gardens. Turning to ask her where they were, he found she'd already left the vehicle and was halfway to the front door.

Luc scanned the street as he climbed out, noted the quiet residential area and vaguely recalled Cassie lived in Seaforth. Although she could have driven him anywhere and he wouldn't have had a clue. Good thing she wasn't out to do him harm.

He chuckled at the thought of Cassandra Moreland being out to do anyone harm. She might be tough as nails and not take shit from anyone, but he knew enough to conclude she wouldn't hurt one strand of hair on his head. Instinct told him he could trust her and that beneath her prickly shell lay a heart as soft as marshmallow.

He'd delved into her life on more than one occasion during the years he'd headed up McDermott Security, and while he hadn't gone so far as to dig up any and all dirt, he did know she was financially secure and didn't date all that much. Luc grinned.

Cassie would be seriously pissed off if he revealed the extent of McDermott Security's probing into her life. And while he liked riling her up, he wasn't about to tell her he'd been poking around in her private affairs without her knowledge. He wasn't a complete masochist. Lengthening his strides, he caught up to her just as she swung the front door open.

"Sorry about the mess. I haven't had a chance to do more than breathe these past few weeks," she apologized as they entered a small living room.

Luc doubted her place would be all that messy. She didn't strike him as the type to be careless with her possessions. "Don't worry about it. I'm sure my place is worse."

She turned and looked at him with one eyebrow arched. "I highly doubt that. You're too in control to allow it."

He paused. How she'd pegged him so well when they'd barely gotten acquainted was a mystery. "You've got me." Luc held up his hands in surrender. "I'm a neat freak."

Cassie laughed. "More like control freak," she muttered as she headed farther into the house. "This way," she called over her shoulder.

Luc followed, his gaze dropping to admire the sway of her hips as she walked in front of him. Not that he could see that well. She hadn't bothered with lights, and yet she made her way through the living room and down the narrow hall with ease. Too busy checking out her ass, he almost stumbled into her when she stopped and pushed a door open.

"The bed's made up. And the bathroom is there." She turned and indicated the door opposite the one she'd opened. "Can I get you anything before we go to bed?"

Her question brought images of the two of them in bed to mind and his body instantly reacted. He'd been semi-aroused for hours now, and the explicitness of his imagination sent his libido skyrocketing. He moved closer and Cassie's breath hitched. Leaning over, he brought his mouth next to her ear and blew a stream of air over the delicate shell. She shivered and jerked back, causing Luc to smile and move closer still.

"I'm good, but seeing as I'm now on the clock is there anything I can do for *you* before we go to bed?" he murmured as he continued to crowd her against the wall.

In the dark it was hard to read her expression, but he could see her eyes widen and her lips part on a puff of air when he pressed his aroused body into hers. Luc wasn't planning to push for more than a kiss, but the second he brushed his mouth on hers all thought fled except one.

More.

Their height difference meant he had to bend his knees to mesh his mouth fully with hers. Widening his legs dropped his head a few inches and placed his thighs either side of hers while his straining erection pressed into her softness, sending blood, hot with need, rushing into his already throbbing groin. He flattened his hands on the wall beside her head so he wouldn't give in to the temptation of grabbing her and dragging her into the bed she'd offered him.

He'd be a fool to rush her. She'd never let him get closer if he used their sexual chemistry to win her over. How he knew that he wasn't sure, but he did. If he wanted to get to know Cassie, spend time with her, he'd have to tread carefully—needed to produce some of his legendary control and back away.

Only that wasn't so easy when her mouth ate at his like she

couldn't get enough. When she gripped the back of his shirt like it was a lifeline. Or when she came up on her toes, arched into him and rubbed against his straining flesh. With a growl, he tore his lips from hers.

"Fuck." Luc laid his forehead on Cassie's and tried to catch his breath. Pleased to note her breathing came in ragged gasps as well. "Damn, you're potent."

"Me?" She fisted her hands in his shirt and he couldn't recall when she'd moved them from his back to his chest.

"Yeah, you." He raised his head a few inches and met her gaze. "You scramble my brains without trying."

Cassie laughed and pushed him away. "Pot, meet Kettle."

Luc grinned. He liked that she wasn't playing coy or using his reactions to her against him. She was a breath of fresh air and Luc couldn't wait to saturate his blood with her. But not yet. Tonight they needed to get their balance, regain some sanity and think about where this was leading. Well, at least he did. "So, is there anything you want me to do? Unpack the van?"

Her smile faltered. "Ah, no. We'll do that in the morning when we get to the warehouse." She ducked her head, but before she could sneak under his outstretched arm and escape, he slid his hands lower down the wall, effectively trapping her.

"Look at me, Cass." He waited long seconds for her to comply. When she finally did, he could see the uncertainty swirling her eyes. "Make no mistake that I want you in that bed." Luc tipped his head to indicate the room beside them. "But I want far more than a quick tumble, and if you're honest I think you'll admit you do too."

She started to shake her head, but he stopped her by gripping her chin in his hand.

"You can lie to me, but don't lie to yourself, Cass." He brushed his thumb over her bottom lip and watched it tremble under his touch.

"I don't have time to get involved. Don't want to," she whispered.

Luc could understand her hesitancy, but he wasn't about to ignore the intense attraction between them. And it was between them, her body told him she was as equally affected even if her words didn't.

"I'm not sure what exactly it is between us but it's far more than one night of pleasure, and I'm willing to wait because I know we'll end up in that bed eventually."

A burst of air fanned over his thumb when she gasped, and a shudder rolled through him as he thought about how her warm breath might feel on other more sensitive parts of his body. Leaning forward, he planted a quick, hard kiss on her lips before he stepped back and broke all contact.

It was the hardest thing he'd done in recent memory, but Luc smiled and said, "See you in the morning."

He strode into the bedroom and closed the door behind him before he could change his mind and take her against the wall.

CASSIE FLOPPED face down on her bed and groaned. Her body thrummed with arousal. She felt achy and needy and empty. Sensations she hadn't experienced in a long, long time.

The last man to pique her interest had made it more than clear he didn't want to date a workaholic, and Cassie couldn't blame him. When she'd first started Are You Game?, her whole existence had revolved around making her business a success. And obviously Jared hadn't been enough of a draw for her to put that aside and satisfy his demands for more of her time. There was no doubt in her mind that Lucas was enough incentive to test her all-work-no-play schedule.

He'd already made her forget the job. *Twice.* Hell, she was pretty sure it would have taken her minutes to remember her own name if someone had asked after he'd kissed her. With another groan, Cassie rolled over and stared at the ceiling.

He was in the room next to hers and he'd made it perfectly clear he'd welcome her in his bed. Only he wanted more than one night tangling the sheets and she wasn't sure how she felt about that. Until Lucas had spoken his intentions she hadn't thought beyond the overwhelming desire he provoked, but now she was forced to examine what she wanted. And Cassie had the uncomfortable feeling she wouldn't like what she uncovered.

Lucas Wilhelm was trouble with a capital T. He'd managed to do what no other man had. Distract her from the most important thing in her life. Nothing and no one had been able to pull her focus from Are You Game? since the day she'd overseen her first event.

She couldn't afford to be sidetracked. Not now that she was launching the adults-only line of parties. Tonight had been a resounding success, but that didn't mean she could relax. Far from it. If anything, she had to be even more vigilant.

She'd taken a huge risk in diversifying in a direction that might offend future customers, especially those who booked children's parties or her corporate team-building packages.

Cassie sighed and brought one arm up to cover her eyes. Worrying wouldn't do her—or the situation—any good, and she'd never fall asleep if she didn't shut down her racing mind. She needed a shower. Needed to wash away the day's grime and hopefully the negative ions would clear her head as well. Sighing again, she rolled off the bed and padded over to her dresser to grab some PJs.

The idea of running into Lucas in the hall had her pausing at the door. Like a thief, she pressed her ear to the timber and listened before venturing out of her room. All was quiet, so she cracked the door an inch to see if he was using the bathroom. No light showed beneath the closed door and she wasted no time sprinting the two meters to the bathroom and safely shutting herself inside.

Although tempted to linger beneath the hot spray, Cassie made quick work of cleaning up and pulling her PJs on. Using the same caution as before, she snuck back to her room and closed the door behind her.

Breathing a sigh of relief, she switched off the light and climbed into bed. The house was warm, the residual heat of the day remained trapped inside, but it wasn't hot enough to turn on the central air.

It would be a waste anyway, she'd be leaving for work in a few hours and she wouldn't be home all day, plus she figured Lucas would expect her to stay at his place tomorrow night. She shivered.

Staying with him would be dangerous. He was already hard to resist, but Cassie got the impression spending the day with him would make it next to impossible.

The floorboards in the hall creaked a second before the bathroom door closed. Vivid images of Lucas standing beneath her shower, his body wet and slick as water cascaded down every ridge of muscle in his magnificent physique played through Cassie's mind like an X-rated movie.

Her pussy fluttered and moisture seeped out to soak her panties. She clenched her thighs, but the action brought no relief from the ache burning in her sex. Cassie couldn't remember any guy producing such an intense reaction, and Lucas wasn't even in the room.

His potent sexuality required no more than a thought to have her panting for breath and struggling to keep from marching across the hall and making him finish what he'd started.

Old pipes rattled as water rushed through them and another spasm gripped her lower belly. She was wound so tight it wouldn't take much to get her off. Her breasts felt heavy and her nipples puckered, throbbing to the beat of her racing pulse. Sliding a hand over her abdomen and into her pants, Cassie zeroed in on her clit and circled the protruding bundle of nerves she knew would bring her relief quickly.

Dipping lower, she spread her body's creamy essence through her folds and back to her clit. Her breathing shallowed—shortened—and she bit her lip to hold back the moans of pleasure bubbling in her throat.

Cassie's hips rocked with her hand as she inched closer and closer to orgasm. She brought her other hand to her breast. Pinched and pulled at her erect nipple and pretended it was Lucas delivering the delicious sensations screaming through her system.

Vaguely, she registered the water turning off and realized he wasn't showering, but she was too far gone to worry if he could hear her whimper and moan as she approached the jagged edge of release. Using a second finger, she pinched her clit and sent herself flying.

A cry tore from her chest, the sound of pleasure unmistakable in the quiet room—and probably the rest of the house—only Cassie didn't care. The hum of satisfaction settled over her, the discharge of tension softening her muscles until every limb—every cell—grew heavy.

Her eyelids drooped, her mind floating on a wave of bliss as the day finally caught up with her. With a smile curling her lips, Cassie thought of Lucas across the hall and wondered if he was seeking his own pleasure.

Luc stood in the dark and cursed. Barely in control, he fisted his hands and clenched his jaw. He'd come close to losing it in the bathroom. With Cassie's sweet scent surrounding him on the humid air, he'd known she'd showered only moments before, which had his imagination spinning visions of her naked in the glass-walled shower cubicle.

Add in the red lacy underwear dangling from beneath the hamper lid and Luc had to douse his head under cold water to cool off. And now, in the hall, with Cassie's cry of pleasure echoing in his skull, Luc knew nothing short of drowning himself in the Arctic Sea would cool him down. He still couldn't work out what it was about Cassie that set his blood boiling so quickly.

Forcing himself to move, he walked to the room she'd given him —not hers, even though a voice inside his head was screaming he should. After listening to Cass get herself off, he'd love nothing more than to go to her and slake his own lust, however, he had enough control to know that wouldn't get him the ultimate prize.

And at some point between going toe-to-toe with the diminutive Cassandra Moreland for the first time and now, he'd come to the realization that *she* was the goal, not the pleasure they'd find in bed together. Which meant he had to get his head—the one on his shoulders—in command of his body.

He stripped out of his clothes and crawled beneath the covers. His cock ached and Luc couldn't help palming his throbbing flesh. With a firm grip, he stroked from root to tip. A shudder rippled through him, and he closed his eyes and imagined Cassie's hand in place of his.

On each pass, he increased the pressure, sped up the pace and in an embarrassingly short amount of time, he found himself on the brink of coming. Stomach muscles clenching, balls drawing up tight, Luc let his orgasm take him and came in hard spurts over his hand and torso.

Cursing his lack of control and the arousal still humming in his veins, he got out of bed and stalked back to the bathroom. Uncaring of his naked state, he didn't even glance in the direction of Cassie's room. Didn't dare—she'd just proven, without being in the same room, she could get to him.

He'd never felt so out of control. Not with a woman, not with his job. Flicking on the water, Luc stepped beneath the cold shower and rinsed away the evidence of his weakness. She'd gotten under his skin—in his blood—and he didn't have a clue how to get her out or even if he wanted to.

With a groan, he closed his eyes and ducked his head under the spray. The water pelted his scalp, the sound drowning the voice in his head that told him to go to Cassie and finish what they both obviously wanted. He had no idea how long he stood beneath the cold shower, but he finally roused himself and switched it off.

Eyeing the only towel on the rack, he couldn't bring himself to use it, knowing she'd rubbed it all over her body first. Glancing around the room, he spied the cupboard tucked in behind the door and opened it to find shelves filled with female toiletries as well as fresh towels.

Grinning, Luc snagged one and ran it over his face only to have the smile die a quick death when he caught Cassie's distinct scent. With a moan, he buried his face deeper into the soft fabric and drew in a breath. Her smell surrounded him. It wasn't as pronounced as when he'd held her in his arms, but it was just as effective.

The erection he'd so recently satisfied re-emerged, and he wondered if he'd ever quench the thirst for Cassie his body seemed to have. One thing he was sure of was this wasn't your everyday run-of-the-mill kind of lust.

For a start, he respected her—admired her—and he could tell they held the same moral codes when it came to working hard and going after what they wanted. She wasn't hard on the eyes either. In spite of her lack of height, she wasn't what he'd call short, just shorter than his usual preference.

Of course, those preferences hadn't found him anywhere near the pleasure he'd found with Cassie, and he hadn't even fucked her yet. He had to assume there would be fireworks once he managed to get her beneath him.

Dry, Luc hung the towel on the free rail and made his way back to his room. The house remained quiet around him and he assumed Cassie had gone to sleep after she'd come loud enough to shake the rafters.

He chuckled. Hearing her scream when he made her climax would be music to his ears. A symphony he couldn't wait to conduct. With a smile, he climbed into bed once more and thought about tomorrow and how he'd win Cassie over. He expected her to fight him—in spite of their combustible attraction, they hardly knew each other—and he relished the chance to tussle with her again.

No doubt about it. Cassandra Moreland fired his blood and went close to driving him insane, but he wasn't about to walk away. Not until he'd explored every inch of her, discovered everything that made her tick and convinced her she wanted to do the same to him.

By the time their challenge was over, Luc hoped to have made inroads in his quest to not only win her over but to win her heart. He had the feeling she guarded that soft center with razor wire, but he planned to breach her defenses, because suddenly he wouldn't be happy with anything less than all of her.

5

Cassie rolled over with a grunt when her phone alarm blared from across the room. Burrowing her head beneath her pillow, she tried to ignore the offending noise, but that only allowed the voice in her head to remind her no one else would run Are You Game? or today's event. Just the thought of a lively bunch of five-year-olds made her want to weep. Of course, once she mainlined some caffeine and showered she'd be right to go. It was those minutes until then that were always the killer.

Eyes closed, Cassie tossed the pillow aside and all but fell out of bed. With her eyelids barely cracked, she staggered the few steps to her dresser and stabbed at the screen of her iPhone until the screeching stopped. Silence. Her lips tipped up on the ends while her ears sighed in relief.

Floorboards creaked beneath her bare feet as she made her way to the kitchen and the coffee pot. The aroma of coffee hung on the air and Cassie thanked the inventor of the humble timer mechanism. She also thanked herself for having the foresight to set the timer yesterday before she left for work so she woke to the much-needed kick-start to her morning today.

She grabbed her favourite mug from the dishwasher and filled it to the rim with the dark liquid that was her saving grace every day. Cassie had never been a morning person, and even after years of getting up at dawn, her body refused to be trained to enjoy the first light of day. With a sigh, she leaned against the counter and took a sip.

Hot, but not enough to scald, she rolled the coffee around her mouth and savored that first taste before she swallowed then proceeded to gulp down the rest of the cup. Warmth filled her chest and belly, and it would only take a few minutes for that initial shot of caffeine to hit her bloodstream.

Topping up her mug, Cassie resigned herself to the inevitable and headed back to her room. She had a lot to do this morning. Unpack last night's equipment from the van, repack ready for the bead party today's birthday girl had requested and do the last minute food prep. Dan would meet...

Cassie stopped mid step, the sip of coffee she'd barely swallowed catching in her throat. Standing in her hallway—naked—was the most gorgeous man she'd ever laid eyes on. Lucas Wilhelm was every woman's fantasy, and here he stood in all his bronzed glory. All she could do was stare. And drool. Definitely drool.

How had she forgotten he was in her house? He moved the bundle of clothes in his hand to cover his groin, but it was too late. She'd already seen his semi-erect cock, and her mouth wasn't the only thing drooling. Heat bloomed between her legs and moisture coated her folds, her body making it perfectly clear where she wanted that magnificent appendage.

And he was magnificent. Cassie had never seen one better. Or bigger. A shudder gripped her as her pussy clenched with delight at the thought of being impaled on his length.

She'd never been this affected by a guy before. Sex—while enjoyable—hadn't delivered this burning need to touch and be touched, and she wasn't all that happy about it. There was no denying the way he made her feel. Even if he couldn't see her dripping pussy he'd have to be blind to miss her nipples doing their impersonation of

Sydney Tower. They all but poked holes in her tank top they were that hard.

Lucas cleared his throat and Cassie's gaze darted up to collide with fiery black orbs. The flare of desire he aimed at her had heat washing up her neck and into her face. "Um..."

"I was going to grab a quick shower." His voice, rough and deep, skipped over her nerves and sent a shiver down her spine.

"Oh, right. Yes." She licked her bottom lip. "Go ahead. I'll go after you and we'll leave in about thirty minutes. Coffee's in the kitchen."

"Thanks." He didn't move.

Acutely aware of his every breath, Cassie sidled past him and escaped to the safety of her room. Only there was nothing safe about her bedroom. Not when she could still see him in her mind, and when the old house's plumbing rattled, she imagined him naked—wet. Sleek and hot as he stood beneath the falling water.

Her breathing stuttered and her lower belly warmed with arousal that dripped down into her core to remind her of what she was missing. There was no way she'd last through his shower. Yanking her bedside drawer open, she put her cup down, grabbed her ear buds and plugged them into her phone.

Within seconds, the pounding beat of the latest dance-floor tune filled her head and drowned out the sound of water rushing through pipes. Unfortunately, the music didn't erase the images her memory continued to play.

Sinking to the edge of her bed, she pressed her fingertips against her closed eyelids and tried to think of all the boxes she had to unload from the van. All the boxes she had to load. The cupcakes she had to bake before ten o'clock. A bunch of five-year-olds high on sugar attempting to sit still long enough to thread tiny colored beads on thin lengths of elastic to make necklaces and bracelets. But nothing seemed to remove the stunning pictures of Lucas in all his nakedness.

Frustrated in more ways than one, Cassie jumped to her feet and frantically gathered clothes to wear. Once that was done, she pivoted on her heel looking for something else to occupy her hands.

Spying her mug, she reached over and snatched it up, causing the dark liquid to slosh up the sides. She took a few quick gulps. Still warm, the coffee went down smooth, but like everything else she'd tried, it failed miserably in its effort to wipe her mind clean of one sexy man Cassie had the feeling she'd never be able to ignore no matter how much she wanted to. With her body humming and a sexy beat pounding in her ears, Cassie started to wonder why she even bothered.

Who said she couldn't enjoy all Lucas had to offer while he offered it?

A relationship was the last thing she wanted. The disastrous end to her last one had cured her of the notion she could have a successful business and a boyfriend. She wasn't the type to indulge in one-night stands, however, their challenge encompassed the whole weekend, which gave them more than one night. Of course, they'd kind of wasted a night already, but that didn't mean she couldn't make the most of the rest of their time together.

Cassie knew she was splitting hairs with her reasoning, plus there was that pesky problem of him wanting more to get around. Surely one weekend would satisfy him. Lust that sparked this hot couldn't be more than a flash in the pan. And what guy didn't want sex without strings?

Cassie smiled. She couldn't remember the last time she'd allowed herself to let loose and enjoy something for pleasure alone. Perhaps that's where all her previous relationships had gone wrong. Instead of trying to make the guy she was with into Mr. Right she should have been enjoying what they had and not worrying about the future.

If Cassie was going to have a fling with anyone it would be Lucas. Something about him said trustworthy. Maybe it was his job. Or maybe it was the guy himself. Either way, she wasn't going to let him walk away like he had last night. No. Next time they found themselves in a steamy lip-lock, Cassie would make sure they didn't stop there.

Luc scrubbed a hand over his stubbled chin. He needed a shave, but that wasn't happening until he went home. He'd been a twice-a-day shaver since he hit puberty, which meant he'd have to be careful around Cassie.

The sharp bristles would leave her skin raw, and while the thought of marking her in that way sent a thrill through him, he wouldn't risk hurting her. She might be a tough little thing, but her skin was soft as silk, and he had no doubt she'd end up with a severe case of beard burn.

He picked up yesterday's boxers and instantly changed his mind, dropping them back on the floor. He'd rather go commando than wear the pre-worn underwear. Snatching up his pants, he dropped the towel from around his waist and stepped into one leg.

With his other foot off the floor and both hands on his pants, Luc had no way of stopping the door from swinging open. Stumbling backward, he crashed into the basin and dropped his pants to catch his balance. For the second time today, Cassie stood in front of him staring at his groin.

Neither of them moved. Well, his cock did. That part of his anatomy knew exactly what to do around Cassie. Her shorts and top may have adequately covered her luscious body, but his libido didn't seem to care what she dressed in. It just wanted to get her undressed as quickly as possible, and at this point Luc couldn't come up with a good argument against getting her naked.

Now.

He noted he wasn't the only one affected by their close quarters. Cassie's breathing was shallow, her skin flushed and her nipples were hard beneath her thin shirt.

Before he thought about it, he had her in his arms. He spun around, hoisted her onto the basin and, using his legs, spread her knees until they were wide enough for his thighs to fit snugly between hers, his cock pressing into her belly. Luc lowered his head and took her mouth.

She parted her lips, and he took the silent invitation and thrust his tongue between her teeth to explore the hot recesses of her mouth. For seconds, she remained passive, letting him do and take as he wished. Then she exploded in a hungry surge that stole his breath. There was nothing submissive about her now. She stroked her tongue over his, past his teeth and into his mouth.

In moments, their kiss turned desperate. Blood rushed in his ears, his heart pounded in his chest and his cock throbbed where it lay trapped between them. He bucked his hips, rocked his length against her. He gripped the hem of her shirt and yanked it up so he could get his hands on the hard nipples that were digging into his chest.

Air rushed from his lungs when he cradled the soft globes in his palms. Luc pulled his mouth from hers and looked down. Cassie's top was bunched beneath her arms and his darker flesh covered her creamy skin. The sight sent an erotic spike into his groin.

He had to taste her. Had to feel her under his lips—his tongue. He lowered his head and trailed his mouth down her chin to her throat. Her pulse beat in a rapid tattoo and he lingered over it. Nipping and licking until her head fell back and she gave him free rein.

She gasped when he scrapped his teeth across her collarbone. Moaned when he moved lower and sucked one taut nipple between his lips. Luc loved the way she arched into him as he drew harder on the rigid peak. His fingers tugged at her other breast while he continued to feast on the one in his mouth.

Cassie curled her hands over his shoulders and pushed. At first he fought her, but she tangled her fingers in his hair and tugged to get his attention. Stepping back, he watched as she wiggled her pants out from under her ass and let them drop to the floor at his feet. He swallowed over the lump in his throat when she whipped her shirt over her head and tossed it over his shoulder.

Damn. She was the sexiest thing he'd ever seen, and he wanted to touch her everywhere. But his gaze was drawn to the valley between her legs. Her pussy hair was trimmed close and her pink folds peeked out to give him a flash of her glistening slit.

Luc fell to his knees and buried his mouth in her silken flesh. Gripping her hips, he pulled her forward so her ass sat on the very edge of the counter and her legs were draped over his shoulders—her heels bumping into his back.

Her smell and taste surrounded him. The tang of her desire coated his tongue, flooded his mouth and sent sizzling need zipping into his balls. She rocked against him, rode the rhythm he set with his tongue and took what he offered and demanded more. He lapped at her folds. Up and down. Back to front. With each swipe of his tongue, Cassie moaned and thrashed above him.

She buried her fingers in his hair and held him close. His groin burned with need and he had to wrap one hand around his cock and squeeze hard in an attempt to stave off the orgasm barreling toward him. He palmed her ass with his other hand, trailed his fingers over her hot skin until they slid through the slick fluid flowing from her pussy and drew a moan of pleasure from her lips. She dug her nails into his scalp and her hips bucked, driving her wet slit into his face.

"Oh God." Cassie's words ended on a gasp as he drove two fingers deep inside her.

Hot walls sucked at his fingers. Clamped down and held him tight as her body convulsed in a bone-jolting climax. She writhed against him, flexed and rolled with each wave of her release until she went limp, spent as the last of her orgasm drained away.

Luc clenched his jaw, ground his back teeth and gripped his cock in a punishing hold as he fought not to come all over the bathroom floor. If he was going to lose his load it would be in the drenched pussy that continued to quiver around his fingers.

He pulled back, glanced up to see Cassie slouched against the mirror behind her, eyes closed, lips parted. She was the most erotic image Luc had ever seen, and he surged to his feet to take her mouth with his. Thrusting his tongue into her mouth, he matched the rhythm with the fingers still buried in her pussy.

It didn't take long for her to be riding the ridge of release again. His cock brushed the back of his hand and he pulled free of her clenching channel to rub the swollen head through her dripping folds.

"Condom?" he growled into her mouth.

"Huh?" Her eyelids opened half-mast.

Luc leaned back, separating their mouths. "Condom? Where?"

"What? You don't have one?" she panted, her hips rocking into his, dragging his length along her slit.

"No. Don't you?" *Please God let her say yes.*

"No." The word came out a sob.

Fuck! A sharp pain sliced through Luc's balls when his brain registered what no condom meant.

Cassie's eye's popped wide and she sat up. "You don't have one in your wallet?"

He shook his head. "I don't make a habit of..." He glanced down at where their bodies were pressed together.

"Neither do I." She lowered her head, laid her cheek on his chest.

Luc slid his arms around her and hugged her close. "Okay. No sex." He shuddered.

Cassie sighed and warm air flowed over his skin, sending a shiver down his spine. His heart pounded hard against his ribs in a bruising beat, an answering hammer vibrated through her breasts and into him. He gulped in air, his lungs struggling to keep up with his runaway pulse.

The heat surrounding his cock didn't help him rein in his lust either. Her cream coated him from root to tip, and Luc would love nothing more than to flex his hips and drive his length into her. But he wouldn't do that without protection.

He loosened his arms, made sure she was steady, and took a step back. "I'll just—"

She moved. One second she was on the counter in front of him, the next she was on her knees with her hand wrapped around his shaft.

"Jesus." Air hissed through his teeth as Cassie stroked him, her fingers curled in the tight grip he preferred.

Her tongue found the drop of pre-come leaking from the crown. She licked across the head, pointed her tongue and probed the small opening as though she were trying to find more of his seed. His groin tightened, his sac shrinking, his balls tucking up into his body. He looked down as Cassie slipped her lips over his head and sucked him deep. All the way to the root, she took him fast only to let him back out slowly as she lightly grazed her teeth over his entire length.

She sank down, took him to the back of her throat and swallowed. Luc's eyes crossed. Fire licked at his balls, blazed up his spine and set off a series of spasms that he hadn't a hope of fighting. And when her fingers teased the taut skin beneath his scrotum he went down for the count. He tried to hold still, but he couldn't. His hips thrust forward—backward, plunging his cock in and out of her pliant mouth as he spilled every drop of semen from his balls.

Shuddering, he held the back of her head in one hand as he locked his knees to keep from collapsing to the floor. Cassie eased back, licking his shaft and sending more darts of pleasure through his groin as she let his softening cock leave her mouth.

Luc gasped for breath, shook his head and tried to clear his vision of the sparks of light flickering in front of him. Too weak to remain on his feet, he dropped to the floor and pulled her into his lap. He pressed his mouth to hers. Thrust his tongue between her lips and tasted his own essence on her tongue.

He kissed her until they were both breathless and desire threatened to overwhelm them again. Panting, Luc broke the connection and tucked her head under his chin. His pulse slowed and his body cooled as he came back to earth. She'd blown more than his dick. She'd blown his mind. Luc couldn't remember the last time he'd had a BJ as mind-blowing or if he ever had. No woman had ever swallowed him as enthusiastically, that was for sure.

Cassie was the first to gather her senses. "We need to go."

"Go?" Luc didn't relax his hold.

"Yeah," she sighed. "As much as I'd love to continue—or finish—what we're doing, I have a business that won't run itself."

"Shit!" He untangled his arms and pushed her back to look into her eyes. "I'm sorry. I should never have touched you."

She laughed. "Don't you dare apologize for getting me off." Unconcerned by her nudity, Cassie crawled from his lap and got to her feet. Stepping around him, she turned the shower on. "You might want to rinse off."

Her words brought to mind another topic. "I'm clean by the way."

"Huh?" She glanced at him over her shoulder.

"You know, health wise. I'm clean and haven't been with anyone in months." He always found these discussions awkward, but it needed to be said.

"Oh, right. Me too." Her face flushed red and she turned away from him, giving him a glorious view of her sleek curves.

Luc watched as she ducked beneath the spray and began soaping up. He smiled where he stood, feet rooted to the floor. A shower with Cassie might not be the smartest move when he didn't have any condoms on hand, but he wasn't about to pass up the chance to feel her wet body sliding against his.

He'd probably end up with a bad case of blue balls by the time they were done. Because no matter what it took, he'd keep a tight grip on his libido and not make her late for work. She passed him the soap as he moved in behind her and he took advantage of her turned back to get his hands on her again.

Hands slick with bubbles, Luc worked his way from her shoulders to her ass. He gently kneaded as he smoothed his hands over her warm back. The water and suds made her soft skin even silkier. His fingers slipped and slid, and she shivered when he pressed a little harder into the muscles of her lower back. Remembering her discomfort the night before, he massaged the area until the tension beneath his fingertips eased. Cassie moaned and dropped her head forward.

"God, that feels amazing."

"Remind me later tonight and I'll give you a full body massage." He pressed his lips to her shoulder. "You'll be softer than jelly by the time I'm done with you."

"Damn." She moaned and arched against him when he dug his fingers into the muscles on either side of her spine. "Why do I have to be the boss?"

Luc chuckled. "I'm guessing that's a rhetorical question."

"Mmm..."

"C'mon." He slapped her ass lightly. "If we don't get out of this shower now we're never getting out."

She growled when he stepped from the shower and grabbed a towel. As much as he wanted to give in and spend the day naked with Cassie, he wasn't about to let her down when it came to helping with today's party. That didn't mean he wouldn't constantly remind her of what they could be doing instead of working.

A smile curled his lips and he turned away so she wouldn't see.

Today would be about anticipation.

He'd tease and inflame until neither of them would be able to deny the electricity arcing between them.

6

Cassie pulled up to the Are You Game? building and hit the button to open the dock door. Metal screeched as the oversized panel slowly retracted into the roof. She needed to get someone out to look at that. Dan had warned her on a daily basis for the last few weeks, but with the business calendar filled up she hadn't found the time to ring the repair company.

"That sounds like it needs oiling." Lucas leaned forward to peer through the windshield at the struggling door.

She sighed. "Yeah, one more thing on my to-do list for next week." Cassie inched forward when the door clanked into the open position. "Another reason I need to fast-track hiring a new supervisor."

Lucas turned her way. "You're looking for staff?"

"Now that the adult party line has launched I'd like to hire someone to work alongside Dan. We're running too thin at the moment, and we've got a full calendar of children's parties plus we've taken on a few baby showers recently that are keeping us even busier on the weekends." Cassie put the van in park and shut off the engine. "It's not fair to ask Dan to work six or seven days a week, and that's what I've been forced to do in recent months."

"I might know someone who'd be interested." Lucas opened his door. "Would it be all right if I gave her your business card?"

"Her?"

"Yeah." He smiled. "My sister. She's been out of the workforce for a few years but she used to manage a fast-food restaurant. Not sure if that makes her qualified for the job, but it couldn't hurt to interview her, could it?"

"No." Cassie thought about the staff scheduling and ordering skills Lucas's sister must possess. "It definitely can't hurt. I'd be grateful if you passed on my details."

"I could ring her now and organize her coming here during the week."

Cassie arched one eyebrow. Was he pimping out his sister? She grinned at the thought. "Being a little pushy, aren't you?"

"Sorry." He shrugged and one corner of his mouth tipped up in a sheepish grin. "It's just that she's my little sister, and even though she's over thirty and the mother of two teenagers, I can't help playing big brother."

"Ah, that explains a lot." She could totally relate to being big brothered and had a feeling she'd get on well with Lucas's sister. "Sure, give her a ring. I'll be in the office every morning except Wednesday and Thursday next week."

She climbed out of the van as Lucas pulled his phone from his pocket. Leaving him to make the call in private, she made her way to her office to grab today's run sheet. She'd get Lucas to unload last night's equipment while she got everything ready to go for today. The cupcakes would need to be in the oven in the next hour or they wouldn't be ready on time. With the murmur of Lucas's voice echoing through the loading area, Cassie took the stairs up to the office level two at a time.

Her desk, like the equipment downstairs, was meticulously organized. Everything had a place and was in it. The clipboard with today's run sheet sat on the top left-hand corner and Cassie scooped it up on her way around to her chair. With a quick glance, she checked her list and reassured herself that Lucas would be more than capable of helping her corral a bunch of five-year-old girls without resorting to duct tape.

She grinned. She'd never stoop to such drastic measures, but that didn't mean she couldn't imagine rounding up wayward children with something other than acceptable means.

"Cassie?" Lucas's voice carried up the steel staircase and echoed off the walls.

"Up here." She opened the bottom drawer of the filing cabinet behind her desk and removed a blank report sheet to fill out to add to the file for last night's party. If she was lucky enough to get ahead of schedule this morning, she might be able to finalize the file for the McDermott party before she took on twenty-four little girls and hundreds of beads.

"Jody said she can be here Monday at nine if that suits you." Lucas entered her office and stood just inside the door. His gaze took the room in with a quick sweep before he brought his attention to Cassie. "I said I'd send her a text if nine didn't fit with you."

She reached over and flicked the page on her open diary. "Nine's good. If we both like what we see I might get her to sit in on our weekly party review meeting."

He smiled. "I'm sure Jody will love this place. It'll just be a matter of whether she fits what you're after for the new supervisor."

"I haven't defined the actual role. I expect I'll utilize her the same way I do Dan. She'll be getting her hands dirty in all aspects of the business." She grinned. "Especially if she's in charge of the new adult party line."

Lucas frowned. "I thought you'd put her in charge of the children's parties."

"Why? Because she's a mum?" Cassie knew she was tweaking his big-brother nerve, but she couldn't resist.

"Yes. No. I mean, the adult parties are new and I figured you'd want to oversee them yourself until the line was established." His brows dipped in the middle, winkles forming above his nose. "I don't know—"

Cassie burst out laughing. He was adorable in caretaker mode.

He scowled at her. "What's so funny?"

"You," she gasped. "As a little sister myself I can almost hear your brain spinning with worst-case-scenario thoughts."

Lucas growled making her chuckle more. "You can't blame me. I was there last night. I saw what went on. Most of the guests were barely clothed."

"The guests, yes. My staff, no." Cassie stood and walked around her desk. "I'd never put any of my employees at risk, Lucas. And while the adult party theme might be a bit risqué, it's not illegal or dangerous. I have safeguards in place for every conceivable problem. You can go over the company's policies if you're worried, but I can guarantee you if your sister works for me she'll be well looked after."

He came toward her. "I'm sorry. I shouldn't question you. It's just that since she separated from her husband I can't help worrying about her and the girls more than ever."

"That's understandable." Now she felt bad for digging at his soft spot.

"Yes, but I still took it too far." He grinned. "It's not the first time and it won't be the last. I'd appreciate it if you didn't mention my lapse to Jody though. I promised her I wouldn't interfere while she finds her feet again."

"How long has she been separated?" Cassie had no experience with broken marriages. None of her relatives who were married had divorced, well, not yet anyway, and most of her friends were still happily single.

"Nearly two years."

"Oh."

"Yeah, overprotective older brother here." Lucas raised one hand. "If I remember right, the divorce will be final next month."

"Then she's probably on her feet already." Cassie laid a hand on Lucas's forearm. "How old are her kids?"

"Fifteen and thirteen. Both well adjusted. Actually, they're all doing great." He sighed. "It's hard to admit it, but they're better off without Colin in their lives. He was never a good husband or father."

"Well then, you're working yourself up for nothing. Besides, I haven't given her the job yet." Cassie grinned. "Speaking of jobs, let's go. You have to unpack last night's equipment while I get today's ready for you to load. And, you get to help me make and ice forty-eight cupcakes."

Not waiting for him to reply, she stepped around him and headed out the door only to remember the clipboard and papers still on her desk. With a sigh, she doubled back, grabbed the paperwork and turned to find Lucas staring at her with his mouth hanging open.

"CUPCAKES?"

Cassie nodded, a Cheshire-cat grin spreading across her face. "Yep."

"*Cupcakes?*" He didn't have a clue why he was repeating himself, but he couldn't get his mind around that one word. He had a very bad feeling about what type of party she was running today. "It's a child's party, isn't it?"

Again, she nodded.

He closed his eyes. "How old?"

"Five."

"Shit." Luc opened his eyes and glared at her. "Boy or girl?" *Please say boy, please say boy.*

Her laughter did nothing to ease his mind. "Girl."

"You think it's wise to have a giant like me around a bunch of five-year-old girls?" Luc wasn't sure what had him panicking more. The idea of being surrounded by a bunch of little girls or keeping his contact with Cassie PG all afternoon.

"You'll be fine."

"It's not me I'm worried about. Most children are scared by my size, and I don't want to ruin the birthday girl's big day." That sounded good. Believable. Heaven forbid she work out his irrational fear of little girls and their frilly dresses. He remembered how awkward he was around his nieces before they hit double digits.

"As long as you don't scowl at them and flash those pearly whites with a smile or two, they'll be fine." She patted his chest. "*You'll be fine.*"

He wasn't so sure, but Cassie didn't give him the opportunity to argue farther. She ducked around him and left the office. With no other choice, Luc followed, mulling over the fact he was willingly subjecting himself to hours of torture. If he were honest, he'd have to admit he was looking forward to every minute of his torment, especially if it meant he'd be with Cassie.

Shaking his head, Luc trailed Cassie through the ground floor. Rows of shelves took up one corner, plastic tubs, all clearly labeled and orderly filled every rack. She led him through a door and his step faltered at the sight of an industrial kitchen.

"You cater your own events?"

"Huh?" She glanced over her shoulder. "Oh, no. This is West's domain. He's Weston's Catering. His company does all the food I need plus he has his own customers."

"West?" He couldn't recall any mention of a guy named West in the years he'd known about Cassie.

"Yeah, he's my brother's best friend." She smiled before pressing buttons on the control panel of an oven that looked way too complicated for Luc to even think about using. "We've only recently added this kitchen. Before that I had to drive two blocks over to pick up all the prepped food."

"And now?"

"West staffs this kitchen when he's catering one of my events, and I use it when I need something as simple as cupcakes." She grinned at him. "C'mon, you can help me grab all the ingredients."

Luc wasn't sure how he felt about this West guy. Something in Cassie's voice made his gut clench. He'd never been jealous before, but he supposed that was the lead weight currently crushing his chest. He wanted to ask her if she had a thing for her brother's friend. Wanted to know if they'd ever crossed that line, and if they had, he wanted to find West and knock his teeth out for taking advantage of his friend's little sister.

He gave himself a mental slap. It was none of his business who

Cassie had been with in the past. Plus, he was fairly certain she'd hand him his balls on a platter if he went all Neanderthal on her. Unfortunately, it was a distinct possibility that he would. All these emotions were foreign and only reinforced his thinking that this thing with Cassie was far more than one night. Far more than a flash in the pan, even though the attraction between them fired hotter than the fireworks on New Year's Eve.

"Here." Cassie handed him a container and proceeded to load him up one after another until the pile reached his chin. "Take those over to the island while I get what I need from the cold room."

His phone beeped as he placed his load on the counter. He pulled it from his pocket and opened his email app, quickly scanning the latest update on the Lachlan and Cameron incident. Nothing new or requiring his attention. Thank God.

The last thing he wanted was to interrupt his time with Cassie more than his job already had. Although he was sure she'd understand, Luc didn't want to risk losing her attention before they'd forged a stronger bond.

"Problem?" she asked as she stepped next to him.

"No." He exited the mail app and stuffed his phone back in his pocket. "Nothing urgent or needing my input."

"I won't hold it against you if you have to bail on our deal." One side of her mouth kicked up. "Promise not to call you a welsher."

He wrapped a hand around the back of her neck and tugged her close. Lowering his head, he brought their mouths to within an inch of touching. "Oh, don't worry. I have no intention of reneging on our arrangement."

Luc pulled her in and slanted his mouth across hers. He didn't wait to be invited inside. Not when a little pressure had her opening to him with eager demand. Her tongue tangled with his. Their teeth bumped in the rush to take—to devour. It wasn't enough. This press of lips didn't satisfy the need, only inflamed it. Fire licked along his nerves, lashed at his groin and threatened to incinerate his thin grip on control.

Lust coursed through his veins and drove him to grab her ass and drag her in against his throbbing length. His hips flexed, rubbing his swollen cock on her belly. Her height limited their contact and frustration raked him. In a move that was quickly becoming habit, Luc picked her up and placed her on the counter beside them. He wedged himself between her legs, spreading them wide to fit his sex snug against hers. She thrust forward, hit the sweet spot and drew a strangled moan from each of them.

He tore his mouth from hers, trailed a line of kisses over her cheek to her ear. Her earlobe beckoned and he didn't resist. The delicate flesh was soft against his tongue. Sucking, he pulled it deep, nipped with his teeth then lapped at the sting to soothe the slight pain.

Cassie moaned, a sound barely more than air rushing over her lips, but Luc still felt it gut deep. It pulled and twisted, tightened his already taut nerves and flooded his cock with more heated blood. He'd burst from his pants at this rate, his clothing no match for the fierce need expanding inside him.

His lips found hers again, and he slid deep. Drew back to stroke his tongue over plump flesh before diving deeper only to retreat and do it again. And again. He made love to her mouth. Kissed her in a way he'd never kissed another and knew he never would. Cassie brought him to this.

To this all-consuming need to take while he savored.

How could he want to gulp and sip at the same time?

How did she understand what he needed and give it to him so willingly?

"Lucas," she breathed his name into his mouth.

A shudder rippled from his head to his toes, ricocheting from bone to skin and back. Jesus. He was going to snap. She'd break him into a million pieces before he ever got his cock inside her. She wrapped her arms and legs around him, clung like a vine, and he never wanted to be cut free. Wanted to stay surrounded by her forever.

Luc's breath stalled. What was he thinking? They barely knew each other. He shouldn't be thinking forever. Shouldn't be feeling the chaotic tangle of emotions bombarding him. Not yet. Surely not yet. It was too soon. Too much.

With a gasp, he pulled away, separated their mouths and stared down at her flushed face. Her eyelids hung heavy over her warm gaze, her breathing ragged in her throat. She was the image of rapture, but he couldn't bring himself to fall. There was no denying he would, no stopping the inevitable, except he needed to think. To breathe. To know that when he sank into the dark abyss she'd tumble with him.

Head over heels.

7

Cassie stared at Lucas. His eyes were alive. The dark-brown depths were anything but cold, and she couldn't get over how wrong she'd pegged him when they first met. She knew he held himself back—he had to in his line of work, except now it was like she'd been given the key to unlock the door to the hidden Lucas—the real Lucas.

She'd gotten behind his shields, past his defenses, and he either didn't want to stop her or couldn't. Both scenarios sent a chill down her spine.

The click and hum of a motor broke the silence as the compressor on the refrigeration units kicked in. Jolted from the haze of lust dulling her common sense, Cassie pushed Lucas away and jumped from the counter, shocked to find she'd been so consumed by him that she couldn't recall getting there.

Her gaze swept the room, avoiding him while she dragged herself back to rational thought. *Shit.* She'd lost her head with this guy so many times she didn't want to count. He wasn't the only one whose walls had been breached.

She closed her eyes and blew out a breath. If he hadn't pulled away they'd be…

Lord, she didn't want to think about where they'd be.

Opening her eyes, Cassie turned to meet his gaze. He stood in front of her, inches away. It would only take one step...a stretch of her arm... *Fuck! Enough!*

What was with her?

Her libido had never ruled her before. Sex was something she could go without easily. Except sex had never felt this good. And they hadn't even *had* sex. How lost would she be when they did?

Her heart pounded and warmth pooled low in her belly at the thought of sex with Lucas. She swallowed over the lump in her throat, licked her dry lips and tried to form words. Only there was nothing to say. No explanation for what they'd found themselves doing. Again.

"I..." What could she say?

One corner of his mouth curled up. "Yeah."

Gazes locked, they stared at each other until the chime on the oven dinged. "Oh." Cassie glanced behind her. "We should..."

Lucas sighed. "Yeah, we should."

He stepped away, taking his body heat with him, and Cassie shivered.

"Right." She needed to get it together. The cupcakes wouldn't make themselves, and the equipment wouldn't unload itself from the van either. "This way."

Cassie led Lucas back out to the dock. She unlocked the van and opened the rear doors. "I'll show you where to put the boxes from last night. By the time you're done I'll have the cakes in the oven and you can start packing the equipment for today's party."

"Yes, ma'am." He moved up beside her to grab a tub and Cassie fought the urge to jump back. With a box in his arms, he turned toward her. "Show me where these go."

His biceps flexed as he adjusted the weight and she took a deep breath as desire rumbled through her center. At this rate she'd be jumping him in the warehouse. Not something she wanted to do.

Okay, that was lie. She definitely wanted to jump him. But she couldn't do that here.

They needed distance. A few hours—possibly days—apart would be good. She'd have to settle for minutes though. With the deal they'd made she was lucky to get that much, so she'd grab what she could and hope it was enough to get her feet back on steady ground. And her mind out of the gutter.

"Over here." Taking a deep breath, Cassie headed for the storage racks. "Everything—shelves, boxes—are clearly labeled, so you shouldn't have any trouble putting it all away, but if you do give me a yell."

"I think I can muddle through."

She heard the grin in his voice and glanced over her shoulder. Not only was he smiling, but he was smiling while ogling her ass. Her step stuttered, a small pause that threatened to have him crashing into her back. Double stepping, she moved to the side and pointed to the first row of equipment.

"Glasses, china, platters and cutlery are in this aisle. Next is prep equipment and then sundries like napkins. Condiments are stored in the kitchen area, but leave those because I think they're all on today's list of requirements. Make sure you put everything in its proper place. The last thing I need is to have to search for equipment."

"Cass." He waited for her to look at him. "I've got it. Go make cupcakes."

Lucas strode past, a smile curving his lips, and Cassie wasn't sure if she was happy or sad that he could function so well after their kitchen encounter. With no time to dwell on her turbulent thoughts, she headed back to the scene of the crime and steeled herself against the memories of their scorching kiss.

∽

Luc breathed easier as the echo of Cassie's footsteps faded. He wasn't sure how he'd kept his hands to himself. She tempted him in so many ways. The stunned look on her face when she'd jumped off the counter made him want to pull her in and hold her close. Soothe

the alarm he'd seen in her eyes. Reassure her they'd done nothing wrong. Only they had. He'd all but screwed her on the job.

Would have if his own panic hadn't forced him to back off. Last night, he'd acknowledged their chemistry was volatile, but what he hadn't realized was his complete lack of control over his lust for Cassie.

He slid the box in his arms onto a shelf and with his hands free, drove his fingers through his hair. Today would be an exercise in restraint. One he figured he'd fail. Keeping Cassie at a distance, one where he couldn't get his hands on her, was impossible. Only he had to try.

Had to get the raging inferno burning between them under control until they were somewhere less public. Somewhere other than her place of work. Or his. He'd forgive himself for this morning in her bathroom but not the other times he'd dragged her against him.

Each time he'd been powerless to stop—a shudder ran through him—helpless in the face of his want for her. She was like lightning. Cracking hard and fast across his nerves. Sending his heart rate into overdrive and his mind blank in a flash of spine-bending need.

He'd never felt anything like it, and he couldn't bring himself to walk away from her. He knew they were bound to get burned. The flames between them were too hot to do anything else. And still he wouldn't take the cautious path. For once in his life, Luc was walking into something without knowing all the possible outcomes.

Shaking his head, he headed back to the van and got to work. He'd promised to be at her beck and call for twenty-four hours and he would be. Even if he had to sit with a bunch of five-year-old girls for most of the day. With any luck, Cassie would let him hang back and not get too close to the birthday girl or her guests. Somehow he didn't think he'd be that fortunate.

He worked up a sweat. The air inside the warehouse was still and as the sun heated the metal walls, the temperature rose to a stifling level. He'd rolled up his sleeves, undone the top four buttons on his shirt, but neither gave him much relief.

They'd have to make a detour to his house on the way to the party. There was no way he wanted to spend the rest of the day in yesterday's clothes. Not to mention he was commando since he'd refused to wear his boxers for a second time.

Luc climbed out of the van with the last box and was headed over to the racks when Cassie came through from the kitchen. She carried a tub that almost blocked her view. With a skill that spoke of numerous trips of a similar nature, she navigated around shelving and came toward him. He couldn't help but return the smile she aimed his way. Waiting where he was, he watched her as she sailed past and slid the tub onto the van floor.

"Oh good, you're almost done." She aimed that smile his way again and his knees actually went weak. "We're ahead of schedule so we can grab something to eat on the way to the party unless you'd prefer cupcakes."

This time her grin grabbed him by the balls. He wanted to see her smile like that all the time. It wasn't just a curve of her lips. Her whole face lit up. Her eyes sparkled and the little creases beside them told him she did it often in spite of the fact she'd never graced him with one this genuine. But it was the dimples that did him in. God, they were so deep. How had he not noticed them before? The urge to kiss them—lick them—pierced him and he leaned forward and took a step before he stopped himself.

She breezed past, a light fragrance that reminded him of sunshine and rain trailing in her wake. He drew in a deep breath, sucked in as much as he could before the enticing smell vanished.

Like a dog on the scent of a bone, he followed her. It wasn't until she looked at him, eyebrow raised, that he realized he'd been so mesmerized by her that he'd walked into the wrong aisle. Shrugging, he turned around and headed for the end row to put away the last box of equipment.

He took a moment to clear his head before he went back to Cassie. She'd already pulled three large plastic tubs from shelves when he returned. The rainbow of colors showing through the sides made him stop. Closer inspection confirmed his fears. Beads. Hundreds of thousands of beads.

He'd been here before. The one and only time he'd babysat his nieces overnight they'd been eight and ten, and they'd insisted he help them make their mum and grandma jewelry. Luc's palms began to sweat as he thought about those tiny things and the even tinier elastic he was supposed to thread them on.

"Please tell me you don't expect me to help make those—" he waved a hand at the box, "—things."

Cassie burst out laughing.

Luc narrowed his eyes and stepped toward her.

"Oh my God." She spoke between giggles. "The look on your face." More laughter followed.

He failed to share her amusement. Crossing his arms over his chest, he waited for her to regain her composure. Only she didn't seem to be calming down. Every time she glanced at him she sank further into the hilarity he didn't see.

With a growl, he lunged forward, grabbed her head and held her still so he could silence her the only way he could think of.

Her breath whooshed out as his mouth connected with hers. He drove his tongue between her parted lips and plundered. She froze against him and he was on the verge of pulling away when she tunneled her fingers through his hair and yanked him closer. The kiss exploded.

Luc backed her up until she met the rack behind her. His body ached to feel hers, but his height made it impossible to get close enough to satisfy the need. Tearing his mouth from hers, he gasped for air as he moved his hands to her waist.

"Wrap your legs around me." His demand was spoken on a ragged breath as he picked her up.

She didn't hesitate. Her slender limbs surrounded him, her thighs squeezing tight when she hooked her ankles at his lower back.

Face to face, their gazes locked and Luc watched as Cassie's pupils dilated until only a thin rim of brown remained. He wanted to dispense with their clothes. Wanted to feel her skin on his.

Tugging at her shirt, he slipped his hands underneath the soft fabric and palmed her back. Heated silk moved against his fingertips and he groaned, closing his eyes as he absorbed the pure joy of touching Cassie.

"Lucas." She gripped his shoulders, digging her fingers in.

He opened his eyes. Saw the raging fever he felt sweeping through both of them flash through her gaze. "God, I want you."

Her eyes widened, her hips flexing as her thighs clenched around him. Heat exploded where her sex was pressed against him. Did she like sex talk?

Luc leaned forward, nipped her lower lip before whispering, "I want to strip you bare. Drag every piece of clothing from your body and take you hard and fast."

She gasped into his mouth and he licked his tongue out to taste her.

"And when I'm done, I'm gonna start all over again. Only this time I'll go slow. I'll touch—taste—every inch of you before I drive my cock deep in your pussy."

"Oh God." She rocked her hips against him. Her sex rubbed on his straining flesh, their clothes doing nothing to mask the heat they generated.

He thrust forward, driving them both out of their minds and closer to release. Their breaths mingled as they nibbled at each other. The rock and roll of their hips grew faster, their urgency increasing with every surge of sex on sex. His cock throbbed, his balls tucking up as he dry humped the woman in his arms.

"Lucas." Cassie's cry urged him on. "Oh God, I'm gonna..."

She clawed at his back, digging her heels into him as she tried to pull him closer. He picked up the pace, shifted his hips and stroked his cock harder against her. She threw her head back and moaned. The arch of her neck drew his mouth and he suckled the pulse fluttering at hyper speed at the base of her throat. It beat against his tongue, the fast beat finding a similar rhythm inside him.

He moved his hands lower, squeezed her ass and ground their bodies together. Cassie's whole body jerked, her hips thrashing as she rode him. Her strength amazed him. Leg muscles tightened as she used them to grind herself to release. Luc watched as she took what she wanted. What she needed. And when she went over—exploded in his arms—like a flash of lightning, he did something he hadn't done even as a hormone-driven teenager.

He thrust against her and came in his pants.

CASSIE COLLAPSED FORWARD, resting her forehead on Lucas's shoulder as she struggled to catch her breath. Heat and pleasure still rippled through her as the final waves of her orgasm ebbed away. He'd blown her mind. Again. They seemed to find themselves in this position every few hours, and each time they came together it was hotter. More intense.

His breath rasped in her ear and she couldn't help smiling. Lucas seemed just as affected by her release as she was. She unhooked her ankles and tried to slip her legs from around him, but he held her tight.

"Not yet," he panted. "Just need a minute before I let you go."

She knew she should be embarrassed by her actions, or at least a little ashamed for using him the way she had, but with all the endorphins flooding her system, she could only feel gloriously satisfied. He shifted, turned around until he leaned against the racks instead of her. Still wrapped around him, she tilted her head back and met his gaze.

"Wow." She licked her lips. "Guess I got carried away."

Lucas grinned. "Yeah, guess you did."

"Should I say sorry?"

"Not unless you're expecting me to say it too."

For a second, she didn't get his meaning, but when a flush rose up his neck and filled his cheeks the light bulb went on. She glanced down, leaned back farther and caught sight of the damp patch on the front of his pants. "Oh."

"Yeah, oh." He smiled. "Understatement of the year."

Cassie brought her gaze back to his. "You know, I don't feel sorry at all. In fact, I'm feeling rather pleased with myself." She grinned.

He laughed. A deep rolling rumble that vibrated through his abdomen into hers. "Keep hold of that thought, because now we're definitely stopping by my place for a change of clothes before we head out to work."

"I think we can manage that." She untangled her arms and legs and waited for Lucas to put her down. "We better get everything packed quickly then. The cakes are almost done. I was going to ice them here but I can wait and do them at the party. That might be better anyway. With the temperature predicted to be high they'd be melting before we got them on the table if I did them here."

"You know we really have to stop doing this." He gestured between them. "As much as I'd like to keep at it and go further, you're going to have to restrain yourself for the rest of the day."

"Me?" She gave his shoulder a shove. "I didn't start that."

"No." He gripped her chin. "But it's your fault for looking so goddamn edible."

He kissed her hard and fast. She was just leaning in when he pulled back and grinned at her. Spinning her around, he slapped her ass and said, "C'mon, let's get going. I want out of these pants."

Cassie laughed at his unintentional double entendre. "Hey, don't let me stop you from stripping."

A growl rumbled behind her, and before he could grab her, she darted down the aisle and headed to the kitchen. She was pretty sure the cupcakes would be ready to come out of the oven. Hopefully, she hadn't missed the timer going off while she'd been going off. Grinning, she raced through the swinging door as the oven buzzer rang. Perfect timing.

Her timing wasn't the only thing that was perfect.

The chemistry between her and Lucas was a thing of beauty. Of course, they blazed so hot it was possible they'd incinerate each other when they finally managed to get into bed. Then again, they'd more than coped without a bed so far. She bent to open the oven door and her slacks rubbed along her wet slit. Sensation fired, her flesh so recently satisfied oversensitive to the texture of her panties—the press of her pants.

Taking a deep breath, she willed her body back under control. The last thing she needed was to get excited again. There was no time to indulge in another hot and heavy session with Lucas no matter how much she wanted to. She glanced at the clock on the wall. Eight hours. It was at least that long before she could throw all thoughts of work out the door and concentrate on Lucas and the amazing sex they were going to have.

8

Cassie couldn't take her eyes off Lucas.

The last few hours had been mindboggling.

From the minute they arrived, the birthday girl had commandeered him to play the role of Prince Charming. She had to hand it to him. After his initial panic, Lucas had proven to be an excellent prince—crown and all. And it wasn't just the princesses he'd charmed either. There wasn't one mother present who hadn't at one stage or other found a reason to talk to him.

She'd never really dealt with the green-eyed monster when it came to a man. But Cassie couldn't deny that right now she wanted to go over there and stake her claim on Prince Charming.

"I can't believe how good he is with Prissy," Margo said as she stepped beside Cassie.

"Mmm." Cassie dragged her eyes away from Lucas and looked at the birthday girl's mother. "That crown does seem to fit him well."

"And I did notice there's no wedding ring on his finger. Is he available, do you know?"

Cassie looked away and rolled her eyes. Divorced from husband number three barely six months and Margo Fernwig Rothers Bennett was on the prowl for groom number four. She'd seen it before, or at least Margo's type, and while she had no claim on Lucas, Cassie wasn't about to give this woman a clear field.

"He's seeing someone."

"Shame. Still, without a ring I'd say he's fair game, wouldn't you?" Margo headed in the direction of her daughter and her latest prey without waiting for Cassie to reply.

Staring after the other woman, Cassie struggled not to follow. Lucas wasn't hers. She had no right to go charging over and drag him away from the female piranha no matter how much the voice in her head yelled at her to go get her man.

She watched as Margo leaned over to talk to Prissy, pressing her surgically enhanced cleavage into Lucas as she did. He shifted sideways. Margo followed. The frown on his face told Cassie that he wasn't any more impressed by the woman than she was. Smiling, she turned back to the food table and continued to top up the bowls of candy.

"Oh my God. I can't believe that woman."

Cassie jumped us Lucas brushed against her. She glanced up and almost laughed at the scowl on his face. "What woman?"

"The mother. She just propositioned me in front of her daughter."

"Ah, yes, well, she is without her usual accessory at the moment."

"What?" He arched one thick, dark eyebrow.

"She ditched husband number three. She's on the prowl for number four."

"Good God. And she's looking at me?" He looked over his shoulder as though he expected the woman to be right there, claws ready to sink into him.

Cassie laughed. "Relax. We're out of here in another hour or so. Besides—" she placed her hand on his chest, patting him twice, "—you're a big boy. You can handle her. After all, it'll take more than some little woman to scare you."

"That's not a woman, it's a damn shark." He stepped closer. "And there's only one woman I want to be handling at the moment."

She gasped when he dropped his head and planted a hard kiss on her mouth. "*Lucas.*"

"Relax." He grinned. "I'm just making sure you both know where my interests lie."

With that, he headed back to the row of tables where twenty-four five-year-olds were plying their skills as master jewelers. He squeezed his six-foot-five-inch frame into a child's chair and immediately helped the girl next to him thread her beads on the thin elastic.

Cassie's stomach flipped and her chest warmed. If someone had told her Lucas Wilhelm could hold his own in a group of tutu-wearing princesses she'd have laughed and called them a liar. Except now she knew firsthand that Lucas was capable of handling any situation.

Margo caught Cassie's attention as she headed back toward her. This would be interesting. From the look on the woman's face she was not happy about something.

"I don't think that man should be sitting so close to all those little girls." She put just enough inflection in her voice to have any one who overheard questioning Lucas's intentions.

A burst of laughter came from behind Cassie and she turned to see several of the other mothers within hearing distance. The pretty blonde that had laughed stepped closer. "Why, Margo, are you jealous?"

Margo stiffened. "I have no idea what you're implying, Sonia."

"I'm not implying anything. I'm stating a fact. Prince Charming just shot you down and then made it perfectly clear who his princess is." Sonia tilted her head in Cassie's direction. "Getting desperate if you're going after the hired help, aren't you, Margo?"

"Well, I never." Nose in the air, Margo flounced off.

Sonia put her hand on Cassie's arm. "Sorry you and Prince Charming had to be subjected to that."

"Oh, don't worry. I'm finding the whole thing rather amusing." Cassie turned to check on Lucas before turning back to Sonia and the other women gathered around. "And Lucas is a big boy. He can take care of himself."

The redhead on Sonia's left spoke, "Oh my, yes. He's definitely a big boy." Her grin was downright wolfish.

En masse, they laughed and Cassie couldn't help joining in. She shouldn't be laughing at the situation, not with Lucas looking all offended and Margo stalking off. Still, from her position, having her temporary employee sexually harassed at a child's party wasn't something she ever expected to occur. Now if it had happened last night...

Cassie glanced back at Lucas to find him engrossed with the beads as deeply as the five-year-olds. Another thing that made her smile. He was so cute sitting there surrounded by pink princesses. She slipped her phone out of her pocket and quickly snapped a couple of shots of Lucas.

Grinning, Cassie put her phone away and went back to work. They'd had the birthday cupcakes and presents earlier, and she'd packed up the remaining cakes in little bags for each of the princesses to take home. The party bags were lined up beside them ready to hand out, and other than the supplies being used she had nothing else to clear away once the party was over. She glanced at her watch. And that would be in approximately forty-five minutes.

LUC POCKETED the bracelet he'd made for Cassie. He planned to give it to her later. Right now he had to pack everything away. The girls were pitching in to help close lids and stack boxes now the fun was over. Surprisingly, he'd had fun too. A lot of fun. He'd never own up to it, of course. But he had to admit, if only to himself, that little girls were unexpectedly amusing.

They'd squealed with delight when the colored beads were plunked down in front of them. There was more screeching when they managed to thread a few glass balls on the thin elastic to make a necklace or bracelet, and there were even more shrieks of joy when he'd helped them tie off their masterpieces and put them on.

Yep. He'd had a damn good time. Well, except for that one glitch...

Speak of the devil. Prissy's mother was heading his way. He was quite amused by little Priscilla's reaction to her mother's repeated attempts to get his attention. If he didn't know better, he'd think the little girl was jealous and territorial, but he figured it was more a matter of not wanting to share.

Prissy—who the hell named their kid Priscilla then shortened it to Prissy these days?—had told her mother point blank the last time the woman ventured near them that he was *her* Prince Charming and she should go find her own.

He smiled. Even saddled with a horrible name like Prissy, Luc didn't doubt that was one girl who would always get what she wanted. And right now that was her mother at a safe distance from Prince Charming. With shoulders thrust back, Prissy marched over to her mother, grabbed her hand and dragged her over to the table where Cassie had set out the take-home party bags and cupcakes.

"Bet you never thought you'd be rescued by a five-year-old pink-tutu-wearing princess." Cassie moved up beside him and began snapping the lids on the remaining containers.

Luc shook his head. "No, but then I never expected to be repeatedly propositioned by a woman at a kid's birthday party either."

"Have to admit, this is the closest thing to sexual harassment Are You Game? has ever encountered." She grinned at him.

He arched an eyebrow. "Sexual harassment?"

"What else would you call it?"

"Well." Luc rubbed his hand over his jaw. "Now that you mention it, perhaps I should put in a complaint."

Cassie chuckled. "Technically you're not an employee. Bit hard to make a complaint when you aren't on the books."

"Hmm…seeing how you're the reason I'm here, maybe I should sue you for emotional duress?" Luc moved closer to Cassie, bent his face next to hers and blew a breath over her lips. God, he wanted to kiss her. "Or maybe you can think of some way to ease my distress?"

Her gaze met his, lowered to his mouth before bouncing back to his eyes. "Um, maybe."

Luc had to stifle a groan when Cassie licked her lips. He also had to move away before he did something extremely inappropriate for a children's party. "You think about it and let me know what you come up with."

Before he gave in to the unrelenting urge to kiss her, Luc picked up a pile of boxes and headed for the van out front. By the time he got back Cassie had stacked the rest of the equipment ready for him to load and was busy talking with the mothers and girls as they collected their goodie bags.

Hopefully today's party drummed up some more business for her. Although he'd caught a glimpse of the huge calendar board in her office this morning and he'd noticed how many events Are You Game? had on the schedule. No wonder she needed to hire more staff. That thing was jam-packed full. Not one day was clear.

He gathered up another armful and made his way back to the van. As he turned around, he found two little girls with arms loaded. Both grinned from ear to ear.

"Why are the princesses carrying such heavy things when Prince Charming is here to do all the hard work?" he asked.

"My mummy says even princesses have to take care of themself," the little blonde—he thought her name was Michelle—said.

"Is that right?" He reached down to relieve them of their burdens. "Well, your mum's right. But when there is a strong prince around you should let him do all the work."

"Okay. C'mon, Cindy, let's go get our cupcakes." Michelle grabbed her friend's hand and they skipped away.

He secured the boxes in the van and went back to find Cassie rolling up the throwaway tablecloths. "Here. Let me get those."

"I've got this. I need you to take the cake-decorating equipment out to the van for me." She indicated two large plastic tubs by the back door. "Once those are loaded we're done and out of here." Her grin lit up her face, her dimples winking, and he was struck again by the need to put his mouth on hers.

Responding with a smile of his own, he said, "All right. I'll wait for you out front then."

Luc grabbed the tubs just as Prissy and her mother came out of the house. Not wanting to talk to the woman but wanting to say goodbye to the birthday girl, he called out as he walked away. "Happy birthday, Prissy. Hope you had a great day."

"Oh, yes, Prince Charming. Thank you for coming and making my day extra special." She raced away from her mother to bounce along beside him. "I wished for you when I blew out my candles at Daddy's house yesterday."

He glanced down at her. "You wished for *me*?"

"Yes. I wished for Prince Charming to come to my party, and you did." She clapped her hands.

Luc laughed. "I'm glad your wish came true."

"Me too." Prissy tugged on his T-shirt. "Can I give you a hug before you go?"

"Definitely. Just let me put these in the van first."

"Prissy!" her mother called out. "Stop bothering the man."

"She's not a bother." Luc put his load down and crouched to Prissy's eye level. "I really enjoyed your party."

The little girl threw her arms around his neck and whispered in his ear, "I love you, Prince Charming."

Luc panicked, his gaze darting to Cassie. She stood a few feet away next to Prissy's mother, a grin of approval on her face. Shame he couldn't say the same for the shark. No, she was shooting daggers at him. He disentangled himself and stood. Patting Prissy's hair he said, "Thank you for a wonderful day, Princess Priscilla."

She grinned up at him, a gap in her front teeth where one was missing, before she took off toward the house. "C'mon, Mum. I want to have a bath with my new princess bubble bath."

Not wanting to give Prissy's mother a chance to corner him, Luc quickly shut and locked the cargo doors and strode to the passenger side where he climbed in and slammed the door. He couldn't see what was happening from where he sat and he breathed a sigh of relief when Cassie slipped into the driver's seat and started the engine. Staring straight ahead, he thanked his lucky stars he hadn't had to rebuff another obvious come on before making his escape. Luc had a new understanding of what his boss went through after being the target of an over-zealous admirer.

"So what do we do now, boss?" he asked.

"We head back to work and you unload. I have some paperwork to fill out, but I can grab that and take it home to do later." Cassie took her eyes off the road for a moment and glanced his way. "I thought we could pick up some groceries and I'll make us some dinner."

He was surprised by her offer and would love to have her cook for him, but he had a better idea. "How about I cook dinner? I am working for you after all."

"You can cook?" She turned her wide eyes to him for a split second.

"I do okay. Do you have a barbeque?"

"No, only the grill in my oven." Cassie navigated them through the late-afternoon traffic with ease. "Will that do?"

Luc could work with that, but another idea appealed more. "Why don't we head to my place after we finish unloading? I've got everything I need at home to make us dinner and you can get your paperwork done while I cook."

The thought of having Cassie in his house sent a shudder down his spine and warmth into his groin. He could picture her sitting at his breakfast counter.

"Are you sure? I don't expect you to cook for me."

"I like cooking, and if I had any hope of doing the paperwork for you I'd offer." He studied her profile. Her mouth was drawn tight in a frown, and he wanted to lean over and kiss her until she smiled again. "You still have hours left to boss me around, Cass."

"I haven't really bossed you around." She chewed the corner of her mouth and he stifled a moan.

"Well, no, but you're definitely the one who's been in charge and you certainly took me out of my comfort zone in the last few hours." Luc smiled at the little white lie. Other than a few minutes here and there, he hadn't been uncomfortable at all.

They pulled up at a red light and Cassie turned in her seat. "Okay, you cook dinner, but I have to warn you I'm not much of a cook so if you expect me to feed you tomorrow when you're giving the orders you'll have to settle for take-out."

Luc laughed. "You can't cook? Didn't you make forty-eight cupcakes?"

"Well, yeah, but that's baking. I can bake better than most." She shrugged. "Just can't cook much of anything else."

"Can you make apple pie?" Luc had a weakness for fresh hot apple pie with vanilla ice cream.

"Sure." The car behind them honked. "Oops."

Cassie returned her gaze to the road and got the van moving again. She drove another couple of blocks before he asked, "So will you make me one?"

"What?"

"A pie. Will you make me one?"

"Oh, of course. I should have all the ingredients at work."

"What do you need? I might have them. If not we can go shopping. In fact, let's do that. We'll go in the morning." He rubbed his hands together and licked his lips. "I can already taste it."

"We can hit the supermarket near my house tonight. I'd planned to grab some things after work today anyway." She turned the van onto the street where Are You Game? was. "Sound good?"

"Yeah, I can pick up some fresh steaks instead of defrosting them." Luc mentally rolled through what he had in his fridge and decided it would be best to pick up everything fresh. He shopped regularly and rarely had to throw food out, but he'd prefer to be safe than sorry, and he planned to woo Cassie with his culinary skills tonight. The screech of metal blasted his eardrums as the garage door rolled up. That thing really needed oiling.

"Shit." Cassie braked hard. "I think it's stuck."

Sure enough, the door had only retracted three quarters of the way up. Luc undid his seatbelt and open his door. "Let me see if you've got clearance." He stood on the doorsill and discovered they had plenty of room to drive in without ripping the roof off. Hopping down, he slipped back into his seat and shut the door. "Plenty of room."

She eased the van forward and pressed the button to lower the roller door behind them. The grinding metal put his teeth on edge and Cassie stuck her fingers in her ears and leaning over, looked through the side mirror.

"Please go down. Please go down. Please go down," she chanted. When the door met the floor with a resounding crack, Cassie dropped back against her seat and sighed. "Thank you."

"Worried?"

"Yeah, I hate to admit it, but Dan's right. We need a new roller door." She turned off the van and pocketed the keys. "Let's get everything unloaded and I'll grab that paperwork."

Luc followed her out of the van to the rear doors where they got to work. They didn't speak, and he had to admit the silence wasn't uncomfortable. He didn't feel the need to fill it with mundane chatter, and he was immensely thankful that Cassie didn't either. He'd just picked up the final box when she spoke.

"I'll run up and grab that paperwork. We'll be out of here in five minutes."

She took off up the metal stairs, two at a time, and Luc stood immobile and watched her cute butt as she disappeared from view.

His cock stirred.

Not that the damn thing had been quiet all day. He'd kept it under control, but there was no denying he'd been semi-hard since last night, and Cassie was the reason for his embarrassing predicament.

That was something he'd never had to deal with before, an unmanageable libido. There wasn't any doubt that she was hot. But she wasn't the best-looking woman he'd hooked up with, so what was it about her that made his chest ache?

What did Cassandra Moreland have that made her irresistible?

9

Cassie leaned against her closed office door and sucked in a deep breath. It was becoming more and more obvious that she was in way over her head when it came to Lucas.

Her body wasn't the only thing wanting his attention.

She'd offered to make him dinner because she hadn't wanted the day to end. The more time she spent with him the more she liked what she saw. He was no longer just a hot body she could get her rocks off with. And that was the problem. She didn't need this kind of complication in her life.

Complicated didn't begin to describe what Lucas was. They'd known each other less than twenty-four hours and he was already the biggest distraction she'd ever faced. She couldn't stop looking at him. And when she wasn't looking she was thinking.

Like now. She'd come up here to collect the paperwork she needed to fill out before Monday's staff meeting and she was leaning against the door thinking about Lucas. With a sigh, Cassie forced herself to move.

She opened the filing cabinet and grabbed what she needed to finalize today's party. The folder from last night was still sitting on her desk, so she picked that up and headed back downstairs. A quick glance at the calendar for next week reminded her she had to be in the office early Monday to get everything together for Maggie and the Bernard job.

Luckily, she'd prepared all the documents earlier in the week so that job was ready to go first thing. Maggie was her top corporate consultant so she wouldn't need anything more than the agenda for the five days of team-building exercises.

Satisfied she had everything under control, Cassie closed her office door behind her and made her way downstairs. She found Lucas waiting by the van and her stomach and pussy clenched at the sight he made leaning back against the metal side, ankles and arms crossed.

He looked so different in his cargo pants and T-shirt. Easygoing and relaxed. Approachable. Mouth-wateringly sexy. The slacks and shirt he'd worn last night had given him an aura of cool detachment. An edgy, don't-touch, don't-come-close vibe that kept people at a distance.

This Lucas looked welcoming, and she couldn't help but be reeled in when he sent her a toe-curling smile.

"Ready?" he pushed off the van.

"Sure." Cassie wasn't all that confident she was ready to face the next part of their weekend challenge, but she wasn't backing out now. "My car's out front. I'll just grab my bag and clipboard from the van."

She flung open the driver's door, grabbed the board from the dash and retrieved her backpack from behind the seat. One thing was certain in her mind. By the time Monday rolled around everything would be different. It already was. From the second she'd gone up against Lucas something inside her had switched on. Something she couldn't get a handle of. She couldn't understand or comprehend how one person could change her in such an elemental way.

Cassie glanced through her lowered lashes at Lucas. There was no getting past how good looking he was or what her body's reaction was to him, but it had to be more than his looks that affected her so deeply.

For the life of her, she couldn't work it out, and that more than the intense physical reaction she had to him caused her alarm. If it were only lust she could deal with their attraction and move on.

But this whole need-to-know-him thing she had going on in her head just wouldn't quit, and Cassie knew she was treading on shaky ground, knew at any second she'd find herself sinking deep.

And yet she couldn't seem to stop from taking step after step toward him. The only other time in her life she'd felt this out of sorts was when she'd made the decision to start Are You Game?. And while that had turned out to be a roaring success, she'd still been on the brink of breaking on more than one occasion.

They reached her car and she hit the fob to disarm the locks. It was pointless to dwell on what might or might not happen. If she wasn't going to back out of their deal and end their time together now then she needed to let the cards fall where they may.

She was a firm believer in fate. Individual choices could change things to a certain degree, but if something was meant to happen it would—with or without her input. Regardless of the outcome or the traitorous path she walked, she'd made the decision to accept his challenge and she'd see it through to the end.

Cassie tossed her bag in the backseat as she got behind the wheel. They'd have to make a quick stop at her house so she could pick up some clothes and then they'd stop at the supermarket before going to his place. Lucas buckled his belt as she started the car, but before she could put the car in gear he grabbed her hand and wrapped it in both of his.

"Cass?"

She swung her gaze around to meet his, and in those mesmerizing brown depths, she saw concern as well as the banked need that had been shimmering there all day. She licked her suddenly dry lips —swallowed. "What?"

"We don't have to do this." He squeezed her hand. "Nothing will happen unless you want it to."

He was right. Nothing would happen without her consent but she couldn't stop this thing unfolding. No matter how much her mind protested, she found herself drawn closer to the inevitable—the two of them in bed.

It wasn't the physical aspect of their attraction that had her worried, and she had the sinking feeling that neither of them had control over the emotional side of this pull between them. She'd just convinced herself she'd follow through on their deal and now Lucas was giving her an out.

She had no intention of taking it. "I know."

Cassie tugged her hand free and shifted the car into drive. She released the brake and then eased out of her parking spot and turned toward home. The dread of a few moments ago was suddenly gone. In its place was a bubble of excitement—anticipation—eagerness to move their relationship to the next step.

Whoa.

Relationship? What the hell? Cassie glanced at him out the corner of her eye. Since when were they in a relationship? Hands curled tightly around the wheel, she squashed her thoughts and concentrated on getting them to her house safely. She needed to take this for what it was. A weekend of mutual pleasure. Nothing more, nothing less. No strings, no expectations.

Except all the lecturing in the world didn't stop her heart from skipping when he reached over and patted her thigh. Yep. Cassie was in trouble. Deep, dark, slippery sides trouble, and she had no intention of trying to find her way out. She just hoped come Monday morning her heart was still in one piece.

Luc cut the feta into cubes while sneaking peeks at Cassie. She sat exactly as he'd pictured her. At his breakfast counter, papers spread out around her, head bent, writing up today and yesterday's reports. He'd gotten a glimpse of the detail she went into and was amazed at her thoroughness.

Not that he should have expected anything less, but when she'd offered to show him her company's policies earlier he hadn't really thought about them—or her business—in anything more than general terms.

He'd sold her short and he had to give credit where it was due. The businesswoman blew his mind. She'd built Are You Game? from the ground up. And from what he could gather, she'd pretty much done it single-handedly. Oh, she'd surrounded herself with capable people to help, but she was the driving force—the focal point—they all took their cue from.

Dan had rung her twice since they'd left the supermarket. First time was to check on today's party and make sure Luc hadn't done anything nefarious with his boss, and the second to let her know one of their employees had called to say he'd be out of action for six weeks due to a broken arm.

They'd spent thirty minutes sorting out what needed to be done to cover the gap and it became clear to Luc that Dan was more than an employee. It had taken all his self-control to hold back the question burning his tongue.

Were they lovers?

He didn't think she'd hook up with him if she was sleeping with Dan, but that didn't mean she and Dan hadn't slept together in the past.

Luc didn't like the way that thought made him feel. She wasn't his regardless of what they'd done since that first kiss in McDermott's pantry. And she had every right to a sexual history, same as he did. Except it didn't matter how many times he repeated those words, they didn't stop the acid churning in his gut.

"Done." Cassie pulled all her papers together and stacked them neatly on the counter. "Need any help?"

"No. Everything's ready. I just have to fire up the barbeque and cook the T-bones." He pointed to the bottle of red on the counter. "You could pour us each a glass of that to sip while I cook if you want."

"Sure." She slipped off the stool and came around to his side of the counter. Her hip brushed his and he sucked in a breath as fire shot through his blood.

He cleared his throat. "Glasses are in the cupboard next to the fridge."

She took down two wine glasses and poured them each a half glass. "Probably best not to overdo on an empty stomach."

Luc dropped the cheese into the salad and covered the bowl. "I'll just put this in the fridge and grab the steaks. Mind carrying my glass out to the deck?"

With the salad in the fridge and the plate of steaks in his hand, he made his way outside. Dusk had settled over the yard and the heat of the day had eased, leaving the evening warm but not uncomfortably hot.

He'd built the deck himself last summer and he was pleased to finally have a guest—who wasn't family—to enjoy it with. Smiling, he pointed at the outdoor table. "Have a seat. I'll get the barbeque lit and have this meat cooked in no time. How do you like yours? Rare? Medium? Well done?"

"Medium rare, thanks." She pulled out a chair and sank into it with a sigh. "You have a beautiful set up."

"It's a work in progress." He indicated the hedge a few meters from the deck. "Behind there is a pool that's in desperate need of refurbishment. Luckily, the bushes hide that disaster area because I won't get to that until next summer at this rate."

"You're doing it yourself?"

"A lot of it, yes." Luc shrugged. "I like the manual work. It relaxes me, and it's more satisfying to sit out here knowing I had a hand in it."

"Wow." Cassie glanced around. "Did you do the decking?"

"Yeah, last summer. Convinced a couple of the guys to come over for beer and food one weekend and got the harder parts knocked out. Then it was a few hours here and there."

"I'm impressed. Really impressed." Her gaze trailed down his body. A slow perusal that had his gut clenching. "I guess those muscles aren't all show."

Luc's gaze connected with hers. Hunger burned bright and he took the two steps needed to close the distance between them. He curled his fingers around her upper arms, yanked her from her seat and plastered her body against his. Warmth bathed his neck as the air rushed from her lungs. He bent his head and brushed her ear with his lips. The simple touch drew a gasp and shudder from her.

Dipping lower, he trailed the tip of his tongue around the delicate shell until he reached her lobe. With a hard pull, he sucked the softness into his mouth and tugged with his teeth.

The moan that slipped from her throat left him with a desperate need to taste her. He slid his hand into her hair and tilted her head back so he could get at her mouth. Their lips collided, their breath mingling as he thrust his tongue inside.

She tasted of wine and Cass. Two intoxicating substances on their own—together they blew his mind and weakened his knees. He'd never understood how men could lose themselves in a woman. Never known this all-consuming need to have—to take. To claim.

He growled into her mouth and deepened the kiss. She dug her fingernails into his biceps, the sting an erotic shot to his blood that drove him higher. It pushed him further into the chaotic frenzy of want and need. His hips rocked, his cock throbbed and his balls ached. She arched against him, her stomach massaging his length. It wasn't enough. He wanted to feel the heat of her sex pressed to his. Naked. Skin on skin. Hard on soft.

Luc untangled his hands from her hair and skimmed them down her sides to span her waist. He dragged her closer, onto her toes, but it didn't give him what he wanted. Palming her ass, Luc lifted her feet off the floor and urged her thighs around his hips. She threw her arms around his neck and tore her mouth from his.

Their gazes locked. Her eyes were glazed with lust, her pupils dilated, rimmed with a thin line of caramel brown. They stayed locked together until the slam of a door caused them both to jump.

Luc's gaze shot to the house. He heard the voices before he saw his visitors. "Shit!"

Cassie unwound her legs and tried to pull from his grasp. It took him a second to collect his wits and set her free. He waited until she was steady on her feet before he headed through the sliding door to intercept his sister and nieces. Luc couldn't believe Jody's timing. Then again, it was a good thing she wasn't a few minutes later.

"Hey, Jody, girls, what are you guys doing here?" He'd have to have a word with his sister about using the spare key he'd given her.

"Hi, Uncle Luc," Leigh and Amy chorused. They ran toward him and gave him a bone-crushing three-way hug.

"I guess you didn't go into your laundry yet," Jody asked.

"No, why?" He turned his attention to his sister now that the girls had let him go and headed for his fridge and the cans of cola he kept in there just for them.

"My washer died this morning. I borrowed yours earlier today. We're just picking up the clean load that's sitting in your machine." Jody's steps faltered. "Oh, sorry. I didn't know you had company."

Luc turned to discover Cassie standing just inside the sliding door. "Cassie, this is my sister Jody and her girls. Jody, Cassandra Moreland."

"Oh." Jody took a step forward, hand out. "So pleased to meet you. We're still on for Monday, right?"

Cassie shook his sister's hand. "Yes, of course. I'm looking forward to seeing what you think of Are You Game?, not to mention the fact that as of today I'm down a staff member. I'm afraid if you like the job you'll be thrown in the deep end."

"Mum!" Amy yelled from the laundry room. "Leigh won't give me the basket."

Jody rolled her eyes. "Duty calls. I'll just grab the washing and be gone."

Luc watched his sister disappear before turning to Cassie. "Sorry, I forget she has a key and to be honest she's never interrupted…"

Cassie laughed. "It might be best that she did interrupt. We were getting a little carried away. Again."

He smiled. "We seem to do that a lot."

"I'll put the steaks on while you help your sister." Not waiting for him to agree, she went back outside.

Jody came out of the laundry with Leigh and Amy behind her,

each had hold of one side of the overflowing basket. "We'll leave you to your..." She glanced around. "Um, did she go?"

"No, she's out the back putting the steaks on the barbeque." He tried to take the heavy basket from the girls. "Here, let me take that out to the car for you."

"Na-uh, it's fine. Between the two of them they've got it." Jody stopped next to him. "Are you seeing her?" she asked in a whisper.

Luc tweaked her nose. "None of your business, little sister."

She scowled at him. "You don't think this will be a problem. You know, you and her. Me, the job." Jody looked behind and lowered her voice farther. "I really need this job, Lucas."

Instantly concerned, he asked, "Do you need money? Has Colin not paid again this month?"

"No, no, nothing like that. He paid, two days late but he paid." She wrung her hands. "I just really want this, Luc. The girls are getting older and I want to be me again. For so long I've been either Leigh and Amy's mum or Colin's wife. I want to be Jody again."

He pulled her close and wrapped his arms around her. "I promise not to screw it up for you if you promise not to do the same. So no sharing all my childhood secrets and I won't share yours."

Jody laughed just as he'd wanted her to. "Yeah, like I know any of your secrets, childhood or otherwise." She moved back, her gaze meeting his. "You really like her, don't you?"

Luc could lie or divert the question but he didn't. "Yeah, I really, *really* like her," he said with a grin.

"Then don't screw this up for you either." She stood on tiptoes and kissed his cheek. "I better go make sure the teenagers aren't killing each other out on your front lawn."

He let her go and followed her to the door. "Do you need the machine again this weekend?"

"No, we're good." She smiled over her shoulder as she opened the door. "No more interruptions."

Her grin told him she knew what they'd been up to, but before he could say anything to argue, Jody slipped out the door and closed it behind her. He cracked it open again to make sure they got off all right. As the taillights of his sister's car disappeared down the street, he shut and locked the door. This time he engaged the alarm, so if she did come back he'd have warning.

With a smile on his face, he made his way back to the deck and Cassie. He'd love to take up where they'd left off, but now that his jets were cooled he'd concentrate on getting food in their bellies. If that lip-lock was anything to go by they'd both need their strength. They'd be tearing each other apart before the night was over. He quickened his step. The sooner he got dinner on the table, the sooner he could satisfy the other hunger gnawing at his bones.

10

Cassie took a final mouthful and leaned back. The steak had been done to perfection and the salad and jacket potatoes had been just as yummy. She'd eaten too much but she couldn't resist when everything Lucas put in front of them tasted so good.

She couldn't recall the last time she'd eaten such a delicious home-cooked meal. Living alone, she rarely cooked, so unless she went to her parents for dinner it was something quick and easy most nights.

"Damn. That was good." Cassie reached for her wine glass and took a sip. "I can't remember the last time I ate a steak."

Lucas looked up, his fork stopped halfway to his mouth. "What do you eat then?"

She cradled her glass between her hands. "Frozen dinners, sandwiches, sometimes leftovers from work."

"That doesn't sound healthy." He popped a juicy piece of meat in his mouth and chewed. Cassie couldn't take her eyes off his lips. They were slightly damp, and a drop of steak sauce clung to the corner. She wanted to lean forward and lick it off. "You shouldn't compromise your health just because you're busy, Cass."

"Huh?" Her gaze darted to meet his. What was he talking about?

"Frozen dinners?" He shook his head. "The preservatives and additives alone are enough to make you sick."

Oh, right, crappy diet habits. She shrugged. "I'm lucky to remember to eat half the time so those preservatives and additives are probably the only thing keeping me alive."

He shook his head. "You should take better care of yourself."

Cassie understood where he was coming from, and when she had more time and energy she did cook, but lately those days had been few and far between. "I cook when I can. Are You Game? has been so flat out in recent months that I barely have time to scratch when the urge strikes." She smiled.

Lucas narrowed his eyes. "Good thing you're hiring more staff then. You need to slow down and look after yourself as well as you do your business."

She nodded. "Oh, I agree, and I will, once the adult parties are in full swing."

They should change the subject. She could see he wanted to say something else, so before he could she pushed her chair back and got to her feet. "Let's clear the dishes and then we can have dessert. I know it's not pie, but the raspberry ripple ice cream we bought at the shop will do for tonight. I'll make you your apple pie tomorrow."

Cassie began stacking plates, but Lucas stopped her with a hand on her arm. He wrapped his long fingers around her wrist, his dark skin stark against her paler tones.

Warmth flowed from his touch, travelled up her arm to seep into every cell and fill her with a need to be touched—everywhere.

Her breath stalled, her pulse raced and heat flooded her core. The cotton crotch of her panties grew moist as her pussy fluttered, clenched with want. She dragged her gaze to his and all the air was sucked from her lungs.

His eyes were black as pitch. They burned with a passion so hot Cassie's body caught fire with just a look. He rose from his chair and walked the few steps to her side without letting go of his grip.

She swallowed around the lump in her throat, licked her lips and watched as his nostrils flared, his eyes tracking the movement of her tongue. The small guttural snarl barely registered before his mouth crushed hers.

Lucas took them deep. Drove his tongue between her teeth and took everything in his path. The stroke of his flesh on hers, the press of lips, the slick slide of their mouths joining in a desperate need to get closer fogged her mind and drenched her system with desire so potent it could never be satisfied. She tore her mouth from his, gasping for breath while her mind reeled.

He didn't give her a second to catch her breath. His lips trailed over her chin, his teeth nipping at the curve of her jaw, his tongue licking at the slope of her neck on his way to the delicate skin beating frantically for him.

Cassie curled her fingers in his shirt, holding on to the only solid thing around her with a death grip that turned her knuckles white. Her head spun, her chest was heavy and her stomach flipped when Lucas took his lips lower.

Heavy and aching, her breasts tingled, her nipples puckering tight as she waited for that first touch. She cried out when he pulled away, her grip on him not strong enough to keep him close.

"No." The cry fell from her lips on a harsh breath as he pushed her to arm's length.

"Cass." Her name, said on a ragged groan, drew her gaze to his. "Not here."

She didn't have time to figure out what he meant. He pressed his shoulder to her stomach and tossed her over his back. Cassie grabbed his waist, slid her arms around until she cuddled the length of his spine. His strides were long—purposeful—as he made his way across the deck and into the house.

In no time, he flipped her upright and dropped her to his bed. Following her down, he pinned her body beneath his.

"Here." He brushed the hair from her face. "Here is where I want you."

Lucas kissed her then.

A slow, sweet, drugging kiss that left her breathless and craving more. She sank into the soft caress. Sank into the sensual pleasure that his lips delivered. Immersed herself in the most erotic kiss of her life as he took them straight into sinful delight. His tongue stroked hers. A swipe of wet heat that drew her in. Lured her deeper into the man surrounding her.

He slid his hands down her sides, curled his fingers around the hem of her shirt and pushed up. With a slowness that frustrated, he worked the fabric up her torso until it bunched under her arms. All the while he continued to feast on her mouth. He eased back, took her mouth in gentle nips before pulling away completely. She couldn't stop the murmur of protest. Couldn't prevent her fingers from clawing at his scalp to keep him close.

He chuckled. The sound was rich and rumbling and vibrated through her breasts where his chest lay pressed against them. "I'm not going anywhere." His gaze connected with hers. "Not for a very long time."

Tangling his fingers with hers, Lucas tugged her hands away from his head and over hers to press them into the mattress. He tightened his grip as he lowered his mouth to hers again. He brushed his lips back and forth, swept his tongue from one corner to the other, never pushing for more.

Even when she opened for him, he didn't take what she offered. Instead, he drove her mad with a kiss that could only be described as PG. After the carnal way he'd taken her mouth before, this maddening, unhurried slide of his lips over hers ripped away every last vestige of self-control she had.

"Please. Please." The plea fell from her on a panted breath.

Lucas withdrew, moved to brush his lips over her cheek, her eyelid, her temple and finally her ear. He breathed out, blew warm air across her sensitive flesh, sending a shiver down her spine, goose bumps breaking out along her neck. He scraped his teeth over her lobe and another shudder raked her.

"Don't worry, Cass. I plan to please you all night long." He rocked his hips, pressed his cock into her sex and sent sensation spinning through her. "All. Night. Long."

He punctuated each word with a thrust of his hips. Her clit pulsed. Her hips bucked beneath his as her body tried to increase the pleasure—sought the ultimate satisfaction she knew he could give her.

Cassie wanted to touch him, pull him closer, but he still held her hands prisoner against the mattress. She fought his hold, tugged and yanked with all her strength. Except she was no match for Lucas. His grip was tight, not painful, but definitely firm, and he held her in place with ease.

Bringing his mouth back to hers, he nipped at her lips. "Tell me I can have you, Cass. Tell me this is what you want," he demanded.

There was only one thing she could say—wanted to say. "Yes."

L∪C STARED at the woman pinned beneath him. She'd given him the answer he wanted, so why wasn't he taking her?

And why did he feel like it wasn't enough?

Confused by his hesitancy, he shook off his thoughts and gave them both what they wanted. Cassie was on fire. Everywhere he touched her she burned. He unclamped his fingers and trailed them over her hands, down her arms. When he reached the scrunched-up shirt, he gripped it tight and tugged it higher until the garment slipped over her head.

What he'd revealed took his breath. Her breasts were encased in plain white cotton. Not meant to showcase, the white cups concealed her from him, only the look was anything but innocent. The underwear designed for comfort and support had his mouth watering and his cock throbbing.

It was the sexiest thing he'd ever seen, and he flicked the front clasp to expose the flesh beneath. No. *She* was the sexiest thing he'd ever seen. Clothed or not, she was a shot of desire straight to his bloodstream. His body reacted to her like no other—*knew* her without ever having touched her.

From the moment they'd met, she had him climbing the walls of desire, and now that he'd touched her—made her come—he couldn't get enough. He couldn't satisfy his need for her. With a growl, he sat up, straddled her hips and ripped his own shirt off. He tossed it across the room.

Next, he popped the button on his shorts, gave himself some necessary breathing room, before shuffling farther down her legs and going to work on her pants. The button and zipper gave easily, and he yanked the pants over her hips and down her thighs. Sucking in a breath, he gawked at the simple white panties stretched between her hipbones.

"Damn." Luc traced a fingertip along the elastic waist. "Just when I think you can't possibly get any sexier."

The shadow of dark hair hidden beneath her underwear drew his gaze. Dampness left the cotton see-through at the juncture of her thighs and his mouth watered with the need to taste her again. He remembered her flavor and he wanted to sample her once more.

Deciding they both had way too many clothes on, he jumped from the bed and shucked his pants. She lay still, her gaze trained on the hard throbbing erection he revealed. Her sharp in-drawn breath, the way she squirmed on the bed pleased him, and he smiled.

He leaned over her, slipped his fingers into the waistband of her undies and slowly eased them down. He'd seen her naked before. Touched her. Tasted her. Except this slow reveal teased him and worked him up more than ever before.

Maybe it was the fact that he knew he'd be buried inside her soon. Buried deep and thrusting hard until they both lost control and let the bliss take them. Her dark curls glistened with her cream, her flesh, flushed pink and swollen, was slick with her need, and he let his thumb skim the crease of her sex as he stripped her panties off.

She shuddered, a moan slipping up her throat, and Luc couldn't wait any longer. He climbed back onto the bed, slid his body over hers and found a home for himself between her legs.

"I want to taste you again. Want to eat you until you scream my name, but I can't wait another second to get inside you."

Luc flexed his hips, rubbed the head of his cock in her wetness.

His balls tightened, his cock grew harder and he angled his pelvis while spreading her legs with his own. Settled between her thighs, he lined up with her opening and pushed in. Tight wet heat surrounded him.

She rocked against him, rolled her hips to line their bodies up better and Luc's eyes crossed as she took more of him inside. Cassie slid her hands down his back and grabbed his ass. She dug her nails in and thrust up, driving his cock deeper, taking him completely.

Her pussy walls scorched him from root to tip, and he prayed he wouldn't embarrass himself by coming right now. He locked his jaw and concentrated on not feeling the delicious sensations bombarding him. She wiggled under him, dug in her nails and heels to try and make him move. But he wasn't giving in.

Not yet. Any second now he'd lose control and all hell would break loose, but for right now he wanted to savor the moment. Wanted to burn the memory of burying his cock inside her this first time on his brain.

"Lucas." She breathed his name in the curve of his neck a second before she sank her teeth into the corded muscle.

He shuddered, his cock flexing inside her, dragging a moan from Cassie and a groan from him. "Don't move." He panted. "Give me a minute."

She didn't hear him or chose to ignore his request, because she bowed her back, arched up and pressed him deeper before rolling her hips and sliding his cock through the gloved grip of her pussy until only the head remained inside. *Fuck!* His body jerked, his hips rocking forward until he was buried to his balls once more.

"Yes. Again." She raked her nails along his ass cheeks. "Faster."

Luc tried to hold back. He tried to keep the pace slow—steady. But he was helpless against the onslaught of Cassie's need. She rocked beneath him. Took control and drove them both to the brink. He gripped her hips in the hope of keeping her still, but she was mindless with lust and continued to fuck him from the bottom. She wrapped her legs tighter around him, squeezed his waist as she used him as leverage to get what she wanted.

Lost in the slick slide of her soft flesh against his hard length, Luc moved with her. Together they found a rhythm that pushed them closer and closer to the razor edge. He powered into her, drove in and out with hard, sharp thrusts.

Sweat coated his skin, dripped from his forehead and down his spine. Her pussy spasmed around his cock and he knew she was close. His own orgasm rode his back, but he couldn't let go before she did. Not before he felt her walls contracting around him would he give in and take his own pleasure.

He gripped her hips tight and rolled until he reversed their positions. Her gasp blew hot air over his ear and he shivered. Letting go of her hips, he spanned her waist and pushed her up.

Fuck.

She looked amazing straddling him, his cock buried deep, her hair tangled around her face and her breasts rosy, her nipples taut peaks of need and her bra twisted around her arms. Luc surged up, latched his mouth on one breast and sought her clit with one hand. The other, he pressed to the middle of her back and held her to him.

Cassie bucked when he found her clit. The hard nub was slick with her cream and he easily established a rhythm that had her hips rocking. He sucked her nipple, pressed it to the roof of his mouth and scraped it with his teeth. She thrash as a spasm gripped her.

One long second of taut, stiff muscles and then she broke like glass, shattering around him in a rush of wet heat. Luc groaned, thrust in and out as she rode her orgasm. It was too much, not enough, and he flipped their positions and pinned her beneath him once more.

He plunged into her. Again and again. His muscles straining, his nerves flayed raw. Hard and fast, he drove himself to the finish line while Cassie continued to buck against him. In a blinding flash, his release slammed into him. Her hips cradled his as he plunged to the hilt one final time and let everything go.

"Cass!" He name tore from his throat, raw and desperate.

And as he spilled himself inside her he came crashing down to earth.

He wasn't wearing a condom.

∼

Cassie felt Lucas come inside her and froze. Oh God. They hadn't used protection. They'd totally forgotten. She tried to catch her breath. Tried to think, remember where in her cycle she was. Oh God. This couldn't be happening. After being so careful earlier they'd screwed up completely.

"Cass." Lucas cuddled her close. "Shit, Cass, I'm sorry."

She knew he wasn't apologizing for the sex but for a split second doubt entered.

"You drive me so fucking insane I totally forgot to protect you." He brushed the hair from her face and she was forced to open her eyes and look at him. "What do you want to do?"

"Um..." She had no idea what to think, never mind what to say.

He took a deep breath. "Look there's no point stressing over it now. What's done is done. We'll be more careful from now on."

Cassie could only nod.

"And whatever happens, we're in this together." Lucas bent forward, pressed his mouth to hers in a soft kiss. "No matter what."

She didn't want to think about what could be happening inside her right now. The idea of possibly being pregnant scared the crap out of her. Actually being pregnant would probably send her into cardiac arrest. Pushing it aside, she smiled. "I'm sure it'll be fine. I don't think it's the right time." Cassie prayed she was right.

Lucas stroked a finger down her cheek. "I'm sure you're right."

From your lips to God's ear.

Her smile wobbled, but she refused to fall apart. She'd never folded under pressure before and she wouldn't start now. And there was no point borrowing trouble. When and *if* the time came she'd deal with it. She stared into Lucas's concerned eyes. No. They'd deal with it. Together.

11

Cassie woke to warm sunshine and the delicious aroma of fresh coffee. Opening her eyes, she found Lucas sitting on the bed beside her, mug in hand. She smiled and sat up. The sheet fell away, revealing her naked torso, and she grabbed at it to cover her breasts.

He chuckled. "Bit late for modesty, don't ya think?"

Heat flooded her face and she ducked her head. "Probably."

"Here. I made you coffee." Lucas passed her the warm mug. "Slug that down and then throw this on and join me in the kitchen for breakfast." He held out a shirt.

She shouldn't be self-conscious. After all they'd done last night and into the wee hours of the morning, embarrassment should be the last thing she felt. "Thanks."

Lucas stood. "I'll be in the kitchen."

Cassie watched him go. His ass was showcased in a pair of board shorts this morning, his torso bare, and she shivered. Heat flushed through her as the video reel of last night played in her head.

They'd used three condoms after that first time, and the twinge between her legs reminded her if the empty foil packets on the bedside table didn't. He'd driven her just about out of her mind. Though she had to admit she'd done an equal job on him.

Neither of them seemed to be able to keep their hands to themselves until complete exhaustion took them under.

She smiled. Her body might have had a serious workout, but even the soreness couldn't take away from the pleasure she'd received from Lucas's hands and mouth—his cock.

Crossing her legs, she squeezed her thighs together in an attempt to ease the ache working its way to a full-on throb. If she didn't detour her train of thought, she'd be jumping him in the kitchen. Cassie put the cup on the side table and then grabbed the T-shirt he'd given her and threw it over her head. The sleeves came past her elbows, and when she stood the hem hit below her knees. Definitely not a fashion statement, but the thrill of wearing something that belong to him far outweighed the hobo look.

Besides, the soft fabric smelled of Lucas. She bent her head, rubbed her nose against her shoulder and breathed deep. Her belly fluttered, her sex clenched. Damn. She'd better pull it together or they'd be spending the day in bed.

Not that that would be a bad thing. Oh no, that would be a very, very good thing. But they'd made a deal and she needed to keep her end of it like he had yesterday. Today she'd make him an apple pie and do anything else he asked of her. Cassie grinned. Hopefully he'd ask for more of what they'd done last night.

With a smile on her face, coffee in hand and his borrowed shirt brushing against her skin, she made her way to the kitchen and the man who'd turned her world inside out and upside down in a few hours of tangled sheets and mutual satisfaction.

Luc turned the bacon over and glanced out the window. He needed to think about today's plan. Cassie would expect to work. Would assume he would boss her around, and she'd be correct, only he intended his orders to make her have fun. From what he could gather she didn't switch off very often. Someone needed to help her remember there was more to life than work. And he was just the man to do it.

"Mmm...something smells good."

He glanced over his shoulder and watched her climb onto a stool at the breakfast counter. The shirt he'd loaned her slipped down one arm, revealing creamy skin and reminding him of kissing the delicate line of her collarbone last night. Luc gulped, had to clear his throat before he could speak.

"Bacon and eggs. Do you want your eggs scrambled or fried?"

"Whatever you're having." She took a sip of coffee.

"Scrambled it is." He turned back to the stove and finished off their breakfast.

When he put her full plate in front of her, she leaned over and took a big sniff. "God, I'm starving." She picked up her fork and dug in.

For long moments, he forgot about his food and watched Cassie devour hers. He loved that she wasn't one of those females who ate nothing and complained about being fat. She'd eaten a few mouthfuls when she noticed he wasn't eating and looked up.

"What's wrong?" she asked around a forkful of eggs. "Do I have something on my face?"

He smiled. "No. I just like looking at you." Luc dug into his breakfast.

"Oh."

Luc grinned wider. "Finish up, we've got a lot on today."

"We do?"

"Yep." He didn't elaborate. Let her wonder. It would do her good to have a day where she wasn't thinking about what she needed to do next.

They were silent for a few minutes, Luc eating his food and Cassie eyeing him across the counter.

"You aren't going to tell me?" she asked as she picked up her coffee mug.

"Nope. It's a surprise." He scooped up his last bite of eggs.

She scowled. "I'm not overly fond of surprises."

"I'm sure you aren't, but I can guarantee all of today's surprises will be good." He picked up his empty plate and headed for the sink. "When you're done come join me in the bedroom."

Luc left the kitchen and an open-mouthed Cassie behind him as he made his way to his room and the first part of the spoil-Cassie day he had planned. He entered the master bathroom and dropped the plug in the big Jacuzzi tub. Flipping on the water tap, he waited for the hot water to come through before adjusting the cold.

She'd winced as she taken a seat in the kitchen, and he figured she'd be sore after they'd spent the night all but swinging from the ceiling. Hell, he was sore and he prided himself on his physical fitness.

He grabbed a couple of fresh towels and laid them on the counter within easy reach of the bath. He'd like to join her in the tub, but if she'd prefer to enjoy the spa jets on her own he'd let her. Today was about what Cassie wanted to do, not what Luc wanted to do to her. The water was halfway when she came in.

"What are you doing?"

"Running a bath."

"Why?"

Luc pulled her into him for a hug. "Because I'm sure you're sore and the jets will help ease your aches." Her face flushed pink and he tucked her head under his chin. "You can either hop in on your own or I can join you and help scrub your back."

She took a deep breath, her breasts pressing against his bare chest. The thin cotton of his shirt did nothing to disguise the hard tips of her breasts. "Join me."

He sucked in a breath. Although he'd wanted her to ask, the idea of spending the next thirty minutes with a naked, wet Cassie had every cell primed and ready. How he'd survive without taking her was anyone's guess. Luc certainly didn't have a clue how he was going to keep this bath from turning into more than a wash-your-back-you-wash-mine event. Drawing on every ounce of control he had, he let her go and stepped over to switch off the taps.

Without looking at her, Luc shucked his shorts and climbed into the tub, his back against the side, he held out his hand for Cassie to join him. His pulse picked up speed as she stripped her shirt over her head.

Her breasts, stomach and thighs were marked red from where his beard stubble had rubbed against her smooth skin and his groin throbbed with renewed need. Not that the desire for Cassie ever went away. Even the second after he emptied inside her he wanted her. She was a drug and he was addicted.

His system had taken one taste, one sip of her essence and craved more. He'd known the second he'd laid his lips on hers in the pantry Friday night. That one kiss had sealed both their fates.

The only question now was whether Cassie would let them have more than one weekend. Luc wasn't about to settle for only two days with this incredible woman. No matter what it took, he'd convince her there was more than a flash of undeniable chemistry between them.

She took his hand and he spread his legs so she could sit down, her back to him. He wrapped his arm around her waist and tugged her backward until her ass nestled snugly against his semi-hard cock. Ignoring his body's reaction to her closeness, Luc picked up the soap.

Lathering his hands, he slid them across her stomach. No inch went untouched as he concentrated on washing her soft skin. His strokes weren't designed to work her up, but her nipples pebbled, her tummy quivered and her backside squirmed against him as he continued to wash her.

He trailed his hands down her hips and over her thighs as far as he could reach before dragging them back up and across her stomach once more. Skimming her ribs, he skirted around her breasts, along her collarbones and up her neck.

She leaned her head against him and a small moan slipped from between her lips. His cock hardened at the little sound, and he ground his teeth and bit the inside of his cheek to take his mind off his own need. She shivered beneath his fingers as he scraped his hands over her shoulders and down her arms.

Luc stroked the curve of her elbows, traced the delicate bones of her wrists and threaded his fingers through hers. She was soft and warm, like molten wax against him, and he couldn't help smiling.

Her skin flushed pink and every muscle in her body was lax. He didn't know if it was the result of the warm water or his gentle care. Either would make him happy. He'd set out to relax her, to give her a few minutes of peace and pleasure and he'd accomplished that with a simple bath. If the rest of the day went this well he'd have Cassie seduced and agreeable to anything he wanted.

And he wanted her.

More than a weekend. More than a few days snatched from the real world. He wanted her in his life and he wanted in hers. It scared the shit out of him, these deep emotions for a woman he hardly knew.

But he'd never backed down from his fears before, and he knew gut deep that he and Cassie had stumbled across something remarkable. Something not many people found. His heart thundered and his stomach clenched as he thought about where this connection could go.

The water was starting to cool and he hadn't washed her back yet. He needed to move things along. There were other things he wanted to do with Cassie today, and while this leisurely soak was satisfying, it was also torture.

His nerves were strung taut, his body tense with desire for the woman in his arms, and it was taking all his effort to keep things on this side of the line. One too many strokes of his hands over her lush curves and Luc's control would snap. With that in mind, he shifted behind her and, curling his fingers over her shoulders, pushed her forward.

"Sit up. I'll wash your back before we get out."

She bent her legs and, wrapping her arms around them, rested her forehead on her knees. Her spine was a smooth curve in front of him and he grabbed the soap to lather his hands once more.

With slow, gentle strokes, Luc worked his way from her shoulders to the sweet little dip above her ass and back again. Moans of pleasure and sighs of breath filled the moist air surrounding them and his cock throbbed with each one. He'd need a cold shower or a quick hand job if he didn't plan to jump Cassie.

Luc didn't linger, although the urge to was great. He smoothed his hands down her spine one last time before gripping her waist and helping her to her feet. "Hop in the shower to rinse off." He stood behind her, keeping his eyes away from the tempting slope of her bottom.

She turned and slid her hands up his chest and around his neck. Their bodies drew flush and she couldn't miss his arousal with it pressing into her belly. "Thank you." Using her arms to pull him down, she rose up on her toes and kissed him.

It didn't last long. And while the brush of her mouth on his was almost platonic, there was no way she could hide the desire in her eyes. But he understood what she was doing. She was keeping things light, not stepping over the invisible line he'd drawn with his actions. Luc smiled and dropped his forehead to rest on hers. "You're welcome."

They remained standing in the bath, breathing each other in for several heartbeats. Luc finally found the willpower to let her go. Stepping over the tub, he held out his hand and waited for Cassie to follow. No words were spoken, and though he wanted to say so many, he couldn't find the right ones. Not when all he could think of were words that would no doubt send her running for the hills. He wasn't ready to be thinking them, never mind say them. Giving himself a mental shake, he reached into the shower recess and turned on the water.

"Hop in." Luc nudged Cassie's hip with his hand. "Rinse off and then I'll grab a quick shower."

She turned to look at him. "You're not getting in with me?" Her gaze drifted down his body to stop at his erect cock.

He swallowed. "Ah, no, I'll get in after you're done."

Cassie frowned. Little creases formed between her eyebrows. Luc used his thumb to smooth them out.

"Just rinse off, Cass." He pushed her until she stepped beneath the warm spray.

Luc might not have wanted to tempt either of them by getting in with her, but he couldn't bring himself to leave the bathroom either. He watched as she closed her eyes and dipped her face under the water and let it flow down her chest. Turning, she ran her fingers through her hair and soaked the dark strands. She opened her eyes and reached for his shampoo.

"Mind if I use this?"

The idea of her smelling like him all day made his throat go dry. "No," he croaked.

She smiled and got to work on lathering her hair. He couldn't take his eyes off her. With each flex of her fingers his cock pulsed, and he hadn't even thought about moving when he found himself standing beside her, tangling his own fingers in her sudsy hair.

"Oh, yeah," Cassie murmured when he dug his fingertips into the back of her neck.

He massaged her scalp. From neck to temple, Luc turned a simple hair wash into an erotic delight. They were both panting and breathing hard by the time he was done. Tilting her head back, he said, "Keep your eyes shut."

"You're good at this." She rested her hands on his chest. "Do it often?"

Luc could hear the smile in her voice, but he glanced down to make sure she wasn't thinking he spent his time in the shower washing a woman's hair. "No. You'd be the first."

Her eyes popped open and the honey-brown churned with myriad emotions he couldn't name. "I'm glad." A smile turned up one corner of her mouth and he leaned down to kiss the spot.

The kiss quickly turned liquid. Heat and passion that had slowly built over the last half hour exploded between them. Luc sucked her tongue into his mouth. He nipped with his teeth, nibbled with his lips. All the while Cassie fought to do the same.

He slid his hand down her back to grip her ass and he lifted her off her feet and pressed her into the wall next to them. She growled into his mouth as his cock lined up with her clit. Her legs slid around him and she yanked their bodies closer.

His cock throbbed, his balls ached and all his good intentions went out the window. He flexed his hips, pulling back until he probed her opening. With one thrust, he drove himself home.

A ragged moan filled the air and Luc didn't know if it was his or hers. Didn't care. The only thing he cared about was slamming in and out of her body. Plunging hard and fast, he took them both up in record time. She bit into his shoulder as the first shudder racked her. As her orgasm tore through her, it ricocheted into him and shoved him over the edge.

The first spurt of come had his brain engaging. "Fuck!" He pulled out of her clasping pussy and spilt the rest of his seed on her thighs. It was pointless, the damage was done. He'd put them both at risk a second time, and even if Cassie could forgive him he wasn't sure he could forgive himself.

~

Cassie shuddered on the final waves of her release. Her chest heaved as she dragged in each breath. Lucas held her pinned to the tiles with his body but his cock now lay pressed against her leg. She swallowed around the lump in her throat.

Shit!

They'd forgotten protection. Again. It couldn't happen again. But something about Lucas was proving irresistible. She'd never been so out of her mind with anyone else. And she'd never come so hard or so many times with any other guy either.

She laid her head back against the wall and dragged her heavy eyelids up. He was staring at her, his expression one of self-recrimination, and she couldn't let him take the fall for something they were both responsible for. "It's not all your fault."

The skin around his eyes creased as his mouth kicked up in smile. "Yeah, it is. I shouldn't have climbed in here with you."

Cassie couldn't let him take the blame, especially when she'd purposely tempted him with her nakedness when he'd said he wasn't joining her. "You can't help it if I'm too tempting to resist." She wiggled her eyebrow suggestively and rocked her hips against him in an attempt to lighten the mood.

Except Lucas's expression turned serious again. "You have no idea."

With the cryptic remark, he lowered her to her feet and once she was steady, stepped back under the shower. He rinsed himself quickly then grabbed her wrist and tugged her beneath the spray.

"Rinse off. I'll get your towel." He slipped out of the glass enclosure and wrapped a towel around his waist. Picking up another one, he held it out and waited for her to finish.

He studied her. Numerous emotions flashed across his face and Cassie tried to decipher them. She couldn't tell if he was upset about their latest mindless coupling or not, but she sought to reassure him anyway. "I'll check my calendar as soon as I'm dressed. I'm pretty sure we're safe, but I think both of us could use something a little more concrete than my memory."

Lucas nodded as she turned the water off and stepped onto the bathmat in front of him. He didn't comment and remained silent as he used the towel he held to rub her dry. She wanted to take it off him and do it herself. Give them both a breather to collect their thoughts, but she couldn't deny herself the pleasure of Lucas's touch.

One more piece of evidence that pointed to her inability to resist this man. Whether their unprotected sex resulted in an unplanned pregnancy or not, Cassie knew she was still in trouble. Lucas Wilhelm was someone she could fall for. Hard. She had to guard her heart for the rest of their time together. No matter what, she couldn't expect to see him again after their challenge was over.

12

Cassie growled in frustration. Lucas had twisted away from her again. He'd been doing it all day. Ever since they'd gotten carried away in the shower he'd kept his distance, and she couldn't help wondering if he was pulling back because of their carelessness.

Concerned about their second bout reckless abandon, she'd checked her calendar. What she discovered put her mind at ease and she'd let Lucas know it was unlikely she'd get pregnant. Of course, they still had to wait to be sure.

It wasn't only his physical withdrawal that had her confused. Their day had been nothing like she'd expected. After their shower he'd loaned her a shirt and drawstring shorts and they'd headed into his front yard to wash his car.

What should have been a simple process turned into a water fight. By the time they were finished they'd been drenched from head to toe and Cassie had needed another shower to get the suds out of her hair. Dressed in her own clothes, Lucas had led her back to his car and driven them into Darling Harbour where they'd had a delicious lunch in a harbor-side cafe while watching the parade of people passing by.

The only time they'd touched was when they accidently brushed up against each other. He hadn't even held her hand when they walked from his car to the restaurant. And now, as they strolled along the water's edge, there was at least two feet of space between them.

She missed his touch—the closeness that had developed between them—and she couldn't ignore the twinge of regret that pinched her chest. If she hadn't caught him looking at her with hungry eyes, Cassie might think he'd had his fill of her and was simply waiting for their time together to be over.

They were slowly making their way back to the car. Lucas hadn't told her what was on the agenda next, and even with her emotions in a jumble, she was looking forward to finding out what he had planned. So far, even with the mixed signals he was sending her as well as her own seesawing feelings toward Lucas, the day had been great.

Cassie couldn't remember the last time she'd smiled so much. She'd overused her facial muscles to the point that her cheeks hurt. And she'd learned a lot about Lucas and his life. He might have pulled back from her physically, but he'd been an open book otherwise.

She'd never had more fun with a guy she liked. And even though she always had a good time with Dan and West, they didn't count. She didn't feel anything for them beyond friendship. With Lucas she felt friendship, lust and a connection she couldn't quite put a label on.

Something deep and absolutely scary.

If any other man had given her the hot-cold treatment she'd have walked away. Cassie couldn't walk away from Lucas no matter how much she told herself she should. Her inability to resist him sent a shiver down her spine.

"Cold?" Lucas moved closer and slipped his arm around her shoulder.

Not willing to admit the truth or give up the contact with him, Cassie lied. "A little. The breeze is always cool coming off the water."

"We'll be at the car park and out of this wind soon." He tugged her in tight against his side.

To her relief, Lucas didn't pull away when they entered the parking garage. Instead, he steered them toward his car with her tucked under his arm. Their height difference meant she fit snugly against him, he didn't need to lean down and Cassie didn't feel as though she should walk on her toes. In spite of him being almost a foot taller, he was the most physically compatible man she'd ever been out with. Not that they were dating. Or that they would.

She sighed. All this mental to and fro was making her tired. Reaching his car, she reluctantly slipped from Lucas's embrace and sank into the soft leather of the passenger seat. Once she was settled, he closed the door and walked around the hood to the driver's side. With the push of a button, the car purred to life and they were soon on their way. Lucas drove for ten minutes before Cassie couldn't contain her curiosity any longer.

"Where are we going now?"

"Back to my place." He took his eyes off the road for a second and grinned at her. "It's time for you to make my pie."

Cassie had forgotten all about his request for a fresh-baked apple pie. A thrill shot through her. If she was making him a pie then he wouldn't be shoving her out the door the second they got back. She knew more time in his company would only make her fall deeper for this compelling man, but she couldn't bring herself to be unhappy their weekend wasn't over. In fact, the butterflies currently swooping in her stomach were a testament to how pleased she was Monday hadn't arrived yet.

Luc knew Cassie was confused by his withdrawal. He owed her an explanation, but he couldn't bring himself to give her one. It was bad enough admitting his lack of control to himself. There was no way he would tell her he couldn't restrain his lust.

Ravaging her in public wouldn't endear him to her, and there was a good chance of that happening if he touched her. He'd seen the sideways glances, the frown marring her pretty face, and he hadn't missed any of her attempts to initiate contact. If they made it home without him pulling over and swooping in for a kiss it would be a miracle.

Mid-Sunday afternoon traffic was light, but the drive to his house took over thirty minutes. Silence hung between them like a thundercloud—heavy, dark and filled with electric tension that had the hairs on his arms standing on end. He'd done that to them. Turned their easy, friendly rapport into a strained acquaintance. He needed to get them back to where they'd been before they'd left his house this morning. Luc could only hope it was possible.

"Is there anything you need at the shops?" he asked, trying to break the unease between them.

"No. We picked up everything I need yesterday."

"Only a few more minutes and we'll be home."

Their conversation stopped and Luc racked his brain for something to say. He came up empty. Cursing himself a fool, he pushed the accelerator down harder and nudged the car over the speed limit to reach their destination quicker. Not wanting to get into a discussion about his behavior in the car, he kept quiet for the last few minutes of the trip. As he pulled into his driveway his phone rang, the hands-free system blasting the sound through the car's speakers.

Luc didn't want to take the call where Cassie could listen. No one rang him except work, and while it was unlikely the conversation would hold any confidential information, he couldn't risk it, so he reached over and diverted the call to voicemail.

Let whoever it was leave a message. He'd get back to them once they were inside and Cassie was busy making his pie. He pulled up in front of his garage and Cassie had her seatbelt off and was opening her door before the engine stopped ticking. It seemed as though she couldn't get out of the car and away from him fast enough.

Slipping from the car, he took a deep breath before he followed her along the path. He fished his keys from his pocket and unlocked the door. The alarm beeped, letting him know he had sixty seconds to punch in his pin code or have the security company notifying the police of a break-in. Stabbing at the keypad with more pressure than necessary, he disengaged the system. Cassie closed the door behind her and Luc activated the at-home mode.

They made their way into the kitchen and Cassie went straight to the fridge to pull out ingredients. He watched as she efficiently set out the food then began opening cupboards looking for bowls. Taking pity on her, Luc walked over and pulled out what she needed.

"Do you want a mixer?" he asked.

"No, I like to do the pastry by hand. I need a saucepan though, for the apples." She patted the bag of fruit on the counter.

"I would have been fine with tinned ones."

"Nope. Fresh means fresh." She took the apples to the sink. "What drawer is the peeler in?"

"Second down." Luc peered into the cupboard with his saucepans. "How big do you want the pan?"

"Medium."

He pulled out the one he thought would work and placed it on the stove. "Do you mind if I go and check my voicemail while you get started?"

"No, go ahead. I'll be fine here. If I need something I'll just open every door and drawer in the place 'til I find what I'm after." She smiled at him.

"Okay. I shouldn't be long." Luc went to his office with the sound of Cassie puttering around his kitchen echoing behind him. His lips curved up in a grin. He could definitely get used to hearing her in his house.

His phone call turned out to be an update on the fallout from Friday night's party, and Luc found himself back in the kitchen watching Cassie roll the pastry while the apples gently bubbled away on the stove. She hadn't noticed him, so he stayed where he was and leaned on the wall. Her hands drew his gaze, or more precisely her long, slender fingers working the mound of dough.

He remembered what it was like to have those hands and fingers on his skin. A shudder stole through him and he had to shift his stance to make room for his growing cock.

The movement caught her eye and she glanced up with a smile. "Are you going to stand there all day or are you planning to make yourself useful?"

Luc grinned. She had asked him almost the exact same question Friday night. He pushed off the wall and closed the distance in a few easy strides. "What do you want me to do?"

"I could do with a drink."

"What would you like? I've got juice, soft drink, water or wine?" He opened the fridge and pulled out juice for himself.

"A glass of wine would be nice." She glanced over her shoulder at him. "Oh, but don't open a bottle just for me."

"It's fine. You can have a glass now and we'll have the rest with dinner."

Her eyes widened and then her lips spread into a smile that lit up her whole face. "In that case, yes, please. I'll have wine."

He selected a wine from the fridge, a sweet, refreshing one perfect for a summer afternoon drink. She'd seemed surprised when he'd mentioned dinner, and Luc figured she'd thought after today he would send her packing once she'd made him the apple pie. She was in for a bigger surprise, because not only did he plan to keep her here through dinner, but if he had his way she'd be spending another night in his bed.

CASSIE SAT BACK with her wine glass cradled in her hands. Across the table from her, Lucas dug into his third piece of apple pie. She smiled. He certainly wasn't worried about eating a whole pie. The first slice she'd cut for him had been rejected.

Too small.

He'd taken the knife and cut himself a quarter instead. There was less than a quarter of the pie left. Her tiny piece had been more than enough to satisfy her, but Lucas seemed to be eating each mouthful like it was his first.

He forked up the final bite from his bowl and eyed the pie dish. Glancing at her, he asked, "You want any more?"

She shook her head. "No, I'm good."

A grin spread across his face as he reached for the remaining pie. He didn't bother serving it up, just ate it from the plate. When he was done he leaned back and closed his eyes, his hand splayed over his washboard abs. "Damn, that was good."

The compliment sent warmth rushing through her. She was pleased he'd enjoyed the dessert. More pleased than she should be probably, but there was no stopping the thrill of delight that buzzed in her veins, or the smile that stretched her lips as she watched Lucas devour every last crumb. "Glad you liked it."

"Mmm…" He rubbed his hand in circles, drawing her gaze to the perfect ridges of his stomach. "That's the best pie I've ever had."

"Flattery won't get you anywhere." Cassie went for humor in the hope of squashing the over-inflated bubble of elation filling her heart. "I bet you say that to all the pie makers."

His eyes popped open and that dark gaze lasered hers. She swallowed over the lump in her throat. "I'm not known for flattery," he murmured. "If I tell you the pie is the best, it's the best."

"Oh." Cassie's hands twisted in her lap.

"I've noticed you don't take compliments very well." He leaned forward and snagged a lock of her hair. Tugging, he pulled her closer. "You make great pie, Cass."

Heat flamed in her cheeks. His praise brought equal embarrassment and delight.

He gave her hair a sharp yank. "Say thank you, Luc."

"T-thank you, Luc."

His eyes widened, his nostrils flaring as he sucked in a breath. "Say it again."

Puzzled, Cassie complied. "Thank you."

"No, no." He let go of her hair and cupped her jaw. "Say my name, Cass."

"Lucas?"

"No." His thumb brushed over her lower lip sending a shiver down her neck, goose bumps in its wake. "Not my full name. Luc. Say Luc again."

"Luc."

He closed his eyes and sighed. "That's the first time you've called me Luc." His eyelids rose halfway and he licked his lips. "I want to hear you say it when I make you come."

Cassie's breath stalled, her heart raced and goose bumps broke out from head to toe. Heat pooled between her legs and her pussy clenched. A few words and she was primed and ready. It took so little work on his part to have her panting for breath and begging to be taken. She'd never experienced arousal this intense—this immediate—with anyone but Lucas.

"Let's get all this cleaned up." He stroked her jaw as he pulled away. "Don't want to wake up tomorrow to a mess like I did this morning."

Lucas pushed back his chair and stood as he piled the dirty plates. Cassie's pulse sprinted and she couldn't seem to catch her breath. How could he say what he did and not be affected? She had trouble breathing never mind thinking about dirty dishes. Her hands trembled and she gripped the table edge to steady herself. He had her so off-balance. He'd been almost chaste in his behavior today, and now he was talking about making her come.

She'd barely gotten to her feet when he disappeared into the house. She closed her eyes, took a deep breath and pressed her hands to her fluttering stomach. Aroused as much as she was confused, Cassie forced her chaotic thoughts to the back of her mind and concentrated on helping clean up.

They'd abandoned last night's dinner for Lucas's bed, and she was mortified to realize he'd cleared up their mess before she'd woken this morning. Even more shameful was the fact she'd completely forgotten about it until he'd mentioned it just now.

Lecturing herself on her shoddy manners, she collected the rest of their dishes and followed Lucas into the kitchen. He was already stacking the dishwasher and he took her handful and pointed toward the breakfast counter.

"Take a seat. I'll have these dealt with in no time then we can decide what movie to watch." He turned away and got busy.

"Movie?" He hadn't mentioned anything about going out. "Are we going out?"

"Nah, I've got a good selection of movies. There's bound to be something you want to see." Luc glanced over his shoulder. "Your job is to choose one."

"Is that an order?" she asked.

"Yes." He grabbed the tea towel from the bench and flicked it at her. "Now get going."

She laughed. "I'm sure our movie tastes run in different directions. I doubt you'd have anything I'd like."

He grinned. "You'd be surprised. But it doesn't matter. I'm the boss and I say you have to pick a movie to watch."

"The boss, huh?" She arched one eyebrow.

"Yep." He tapped his watch. "It's still my twenty-four hours."

Cassie waited for him to continue but he only turned back to the dirty dishes and finished loading the washer. She wandered over to the family room. A large TV mounted on the wall dominated the left side of the room and a big sectional lounge filled the opposite one. The wall across from the entry was covered in bookshelves filled with books and movies. Walking over she began to scan Lucas's selection.

"Find anything yet?" She hadn't heard him come up behind her.

"Yeah, but I doubt you'll agree with my choice."

"I told you, it's your choice." He cupped his hands on her shoulders and she leaned back into him. "Which one did you want?"

"*An American President.*"

"Excellent movie." Lucas stepped around her and grabbed the DVD from the shelf. "Do you want another glass of wine? Popcorn?"

Cassie groaned. "I couldn't eat another bite of food if you held me down and shoved it in my mouth, and I think I've had my quota of wine today already. I've had three glasses to your two."

He waggled his eyebrows. "All part of my plan to take advantage of you."

Laughing, she walked over to the couch. "I think you've proved you don't need to get me drunk to do that."

Lucas grinned at her before turning to the complicated looking system beside the TV. It took him only seconds to load the disc and join her on the most comfortable couch she'd ever sat on.

"Ready?" He held the remote in his hand.

"Yep."

He pressed a few buttons and not only did the movie start playing but the lights dimmed as well. "Wow. That's cool."

Shrugging he said, "What can I say? I'm into gadgets."

Cassie smiled. What guy wasn't? She snuggled down next to Lucas and waited for the movie to start. She'd watched *An American President* at least a dozen times, but it never failed to pull her in and make her all gooey and romantic. Unfortunately, tonight wasn't like every other time she'd seen it. Tonight all she could think about—concentrate on—was the man next to her and the heat radiating off his body.

He wrapped his arm around her and she sank into his cozy warmth. Relaxed, Cassie let the anxiety of earlier go and soon found her eyelids drooping. Cuddled up next to Lucas, she slowly slipped off to sleep.

13

Luc skimmed a finger down Cassie's cheek. She twitched but didn't wake. She'd fallen asleep halfway through the movie and he'd decided not to wake her in favor of sitting through the rest of the film with her curled up next to him.

He was selfish enough to not want to give up the pleasure of having her asleep beside him, not to mention the trust she showed by doing so. After last night and today he'd wondered if perhaps she didn't feel the same deep connection he did, or had he destroyed it with his mixed signals?

He'd confused her today. Hell, he'd confused himself too.

He couldn't explain the reasoning behind his behavior because what had seemed the right thing earlier in hindsight appeared completely wrong. He'd complicated the situation by trying to manage it. From now on he'd think less and act more. Speaking of acting.

"Cass," he whispered in her ear. "Time for bed, baby."

"Hmm..." She turned her face into his chest.

"C'mon, sleepyhead." Luc scooped her up in his arms and stood. "Let's go to bed."

She wrapped her arms around his neck and nuzzled his throat, her lips warm against his skin. He tried to concentrate on making it to his room and not on the hot woman in his arms. Once they hit the bed though, all bets were off and he'd be all over her. She'd soon be wide-awake.

"Lucas?" Her words were rough with sleep.

"Yeah."

"I should go home. We both have work tomorrow."

His grip tightened. "Not on your life, sweetheart. You still owe me a few hours."

"Oh."

She didn't attempt to get out of his hold and Luc took that as a good sign. And right now he would take whatever he could get because he had a horrible feeling Cassie was going to use every argument she could think of to end their time together for good the minute their challenge was over.

Luc lowered her to his bed and stepped back. "Hop under the covers while I go lock up the house."

He left the room without looking back. The sight of Cassie in his bed would stop him from walking away, even if it was only to shut the house down for the night, he didn't think he could pull himself away from her all sleep-tousled on his sheets.

Luc made quick work of closing the deck doors and then switching off lights. Lastly, he set the alarm to sleep mode and was back in his room as Cassie climbed beneath the covers. A flash of bare thigh had his cock aching and his fists clenching.

Luc would love nothing more than making Cassie more than a little rumpled, but if all she wanted was to go back to sleep he'd grit his teeth and bite his cheek for the duration. Of course, he'd wrap his arms around her and try to convince her it was worth staying awake for a few hours yet.

With a grin, he whipped his shirt up over his head and shucked his pants. Cassie stared at him with wide eyes, her gaze glued to his rapidly filling erection. Naked, he walked to the bed and slid in beside her.

The big king-size bed meant that she was too far away, so he reached over and dragged her close. She didn't protest and he took advantage. Slipping his arms around her, he turned her so her back was to his front. Spooned together, he took a moment to savor the sensation of having her in his arms.

It didn't take long for desire to take over. He started slow, running his hands over her stomach and along her ribs in sweeping caresses that were designed to inflame. When her ass began to wiggle against his groin, he knew his attention was accomplishing its purpose.

He moved his hand up and palmed her breast. The nipple puckered tight and pressed into his palm. He trailed his other hand down her side, over her hip and into the dip between thigh and body.

A sweet little moan slipped from her throat and egged him on. Moving lower, he found her slit, wet with need, and wiggled a finger between her folds. She was slick and hot to the touch, and he was helpless to stop his hips from rocking into her ass.

She thrust back and he lost all thought of going slow. Gripping her thigh, Luc raised her leg and slid his cock along her pussy from behind. Her head arched back, and another sultry moan broke free. His sac tightened, drawing his balls up into his body in preparation for release.

He flexed his pelvis in several fast pumps that drove his shaft through her silken folds and spread her juices over both of them. Heat scorched his skin, spread through him like wildfire, and he knew in seconds his control would be a thing of the past.

Withdrawing, he leaned back and reached for one of the condoms he'd dumped on the bedside table earlier. He tore open the packet and sheathed himself in record time. Ready, he spooned behind Cassie and pulled her leg over his once more.

Angling his hips, he lined his head up with her drenched opening and drove forward in one hard thrust. She cried out, the sound ripping from her as her walls clamped around him.

He held still, buried to the hilt as he searched out the hard knot of nerves between her legs with his fingers. She pushed back against him and Luc moved with slow, steady strokes. Circling his fingertips on her clit and thrusting his cock into her soon had them both breathing hard and wanting more.

Cassie bucked, her hips thrashing back and forth as she worked herself up on his hand and cock in turn. Her gaspy breaths and sexy cries of pleasure drove him closer to the edge, but he held back, wanting her to reach the peak before him—waiting for her pussy to milk him of his orgasm.

"Luc," she cried out as she went over.

Her climax hit her hard and fast, slamming into her with such force that she almost dislodged his cock as her body undulated with each spasm. Heat—wet and slick—flowed over his shaft, easing the glide of his length as he drove it in and out of her body.

He gripped her hips and rolled until he pinned her beneath him. He dug his fingers into her soft flesh as he rammed himself in and out of her clenching pussy. Five quick thrusts and he was coming undone, filling the condom with spurt after spurt of come.

Spent, he collapsed forward. At the last second, he dropped his elbows to the bed and held his weight off her. Breathing hard, he tried to clear his mind and instruct his muscles to move. He forced himself into action and pulled from Cassie's still-quivering body, both of them making a cry of distress as their bodies separated.

He'd love to remain inside her until they drifted off to sleep but he needed to dispose of the used condom or wearing it would be pointless.

Luc headed to his en suite and dropped the rubber in the bin. He cleaned up and then grabbed a washcloth and dampened it with warm water. When he returned to Cassie he found her exactly where he'd left her. Face down with her beautiful rear end on full display. Smoothing his hand over the sleek curve of one cheek, he tapped her hip to get her to turn over.

"Let me get you cleaned up."

She mumbled something he didn't catch but rolled over. Luc parted her legs and wiped the cloth over her well-loved folds before tossing it aside and climbing back into bed with her. He pulled Cassie into his arms and tugged the covers over them. Her breasts were pressed into his side, her head rested on his shoulder and one leg lay draped over his.

A smile curled his mouth. This was exactly where he wanted to be. *She* was exactly where he wanted her to be. Now he just had to convince her it was what she wanted—where she belonged.

CASSIE WOKE in the pre-dawn light and attempted to roll over, except something held her pinned to the bed. Lucas. He had one arm thrown over her waist, his chest plastered against her spine and his morning erection pressed between her ass cheeks. Aroused and embarrassed by their intimate position, she felt heat flood her face.

She tried to wiggle out of his grasp but the man wasn't budging, not without considerable effort, and after all they'd done she wasn't ready to face him yet.

So she lay there contemplating their weekend. Their challenge hadn't really been a challenge. They'd simply hung out together.

There was no bossing each other around and certainly no toes had been stepped on like she'd imaged when they'd shaken on the deal. She was forced to admit spending time with Lucas had been more than fun.

It had felt natural—right.

She'd never expected them to hit it off the way they had. Never expected this deep connection with someone who before Friday night had been a stranger.

She wasn't looking for a relationship, didn't have time with everything going on at work. Only Cassie couldn't bring herself to think about leaving him and never seeing him again. The thought alone produced a twinge in her chest and a heaviness that felt distinctly like sadness—regret. He'd made it clear he wanted more than one night, but did that mean he wanted more than the weekend?

"Stop thinking so hard." Lucas's deep voice rumbled in her ear, his warm breath bathing her neck. "It's too early to be awake."

Cassie smiled. "It's not that early. And I need to get home before going to work so I can't lie about in bed all morning."

"Ha, it's not even morning. Go back to sleep." He pulled her tighter against him.

She sighed. "I really do need to go soon."

"Not yet." He nuzzled the slope of skin beneath her ear. "Let me enjoy this pleasure a little while longer."

With no desire to leave his embrace, Cassie settled more fully against him. "Fine, but if I don't get out of here on time you're in trouble."

"Trouble? What kind of trouble?" He dragged his teeth over her ear and sent a shiver down her spine. "I can think of *all* kinds of trouble we could get into."

In spite of his deliberate twist to the subject, Cassie smiled. She could think of all kinds of trouble too. Starting with the hot rod of flesh poking her in the ass. Not wanting their time to end without one more taste of Lucas, she spun around and pushed him to his back.

Catching him by surprise, she was straddling his hips before he knew what hit him. Giving him no time to protest or take control, she took his mouth with hers and rocked her pussy on his cock.

He groaned into her mouth as he thrust his tongue deep. She tangled her tongue with his while she mapped his sculpted chest and abs with her hands. The man was to die for yummy and Cassie wanted to lick every inch of him.

Her pulse sped up and her blood heated, rushing through her body at lightning speed. It happened every time they came together. Each joining only increased the craving instead of satisfying it. She'd already had all of him and yet she yearned for more.

Cassie traced his bottom lip with her tongue, scraped it with her teeth and pulled it into her mouth to suckle. He let her have her way.

For long moments, she controlled their kiss until her thirst for more of him drove her to take her lips on a journey over his stubbled chin, down the strong column of his throat to the broad expanse of his chest. She breathed in his scent as she made her way to the flat brown nipple nestled within the smattering of dark hair. Flicking with the tip of her tongue, she soon had the small disc puckering tight.

Lucas moaned and drove his fingers through her hair when she moved over to his other nipple and lavished it with the same attention. His cock grew harder where it rested against her stomach and Cassie pressed into him to add to his pleasure. He groaned and rocked his hips up, thrusting his length back and forth over her skin. She wanted to taste him. Wanted to wrap her lips around the head and suck him deep until he was lodged in her throat.

She raised her head and caught his gaze. With their eyes locked, she crawled down his body until her mouth hovered over his engorged cock. Breathing deep, she inhaled his masculine scent. It was stronger here—more potent. Her insides quivered at the tempting aroma and her mouth watered with anticipation of his taste.

Lucas's gaze clung to hers as Cassie lowered her head and pressed a closed-mouth kiss on the swollen crown. Liquid beaded in the slit and, never taking her eyes off his, she lapped it up with the flat of her tongue.

He tightened his fingers in her hair, tugging the strands and sending a zap of pain shooting over her scalp. The sting shuddered through her and settled in her belly, curling deep and contracting muscles as desire burned hotter. She slipped her lips around the head and closed her eyes at the taste and feel of him on her tongue.

Sucking hard, Cassie took him to the back of her throat in a quick slide before instantly reversing until her lips once again surrounded the mushroom tip. Fast lashes of her tongue along the sensitive rim drew a staggered breath and bucking hips.

She repeated the action. Again and again. With each stroke, she pulled him closer to release and Cassie's own arousal climbed. Her cheeks hollowed when she sucked him deep, her teeth grazed as she let him out and all the while her tongue caressed every inch of his shaft.

Cassie brought her hand up to cup his balls. Squeezing gently, she tugged and fondled until Lucas's breath was no more than ragged pants and his hand tangled in her hair. His cock pulsed against her tongue and he yanked on her hair. Hard.

"Stop," he gasped. "Shit. Stop. I want to be inside you when I come."

Cassie's lips barely cleared his flesh when he grabbed her arms and flipped her over onto her back. He came down on top of her, his hips settling between hers, his hot length pressed into the folds of her drenched pussy, and she widened her legs farther. She arched, rubbed her needy pussy against his erection and, with her hands on his head, dragged his mouth down to hers.

She wasn't in control this time. Lucas took with wicked greed. He left nothing untouched, allowed nothing but surrender to his demands, and Cassie reveled in his need for her. Basked in the pure hunger he refused to hide. He gripped her hips, tilted them to his liking as he rocked his pelvis into hers. Her pussy wept as he thrust his cock along her slick folds. Lucas pulled his mouth from hers.

"Condom." He indicated the bedside table with his head. "Now."

Cassie reached over and grabbed a foil packet. She tore it open and Lucas snatched the protection from her hand. He pushed to his knees between her legs and sheathed himself quickly. She'd barely taken a breath—blinked—when he was back on top of her, thrusting his cock deep in one smooth stroke. Buried to the hilt, Lucas gazed down at her, emotions she didn't want to acknowledge burning in his eyes.

She closed her eyes and tucked her face into his neck. Flexing her hips, she urged him to move and tried to pretend this was nothing more than great sex, a physical connection that didn't go beneath the surface. But as Lucas drove in and out of her clutching body, Cassie knew she was lying.

"Look at me, Cass." Lucas stopped moving and brushed his fingers over her cheek.

He kept up the gentle caress on her face and Cassie had no choice but to do as he asked. Taking a deep breath, she leaned her head back and raised her eyes to his.

"Don't." He dropped a kiss on her forehead. "Don't overthink this, just enjoy it for what it is, Cass, no strings, no pressure."

No matter what he said, his gaze told her there were strings and they were tangled around the blazing desire consuming them. She licked her lips and Lucas's eyes followed the action, dilating until they appeared jet-black.

"But—"

He placed his finger over her mouth. "No buts, not now."

Cassie wanted to argue. Wanted to clear the air. Make sure they both knew where this was going. Where it wasn't. Except she didn't know where this was headed. She had no clue what all these conflicting emotions churning inside her were.

She nodded and pulled his hand away, leaned up and pressed her mouth to his. It was all he needed to take them out of the emotionally charged moment and back to the mind-blowing pleasure.

His lips ate at hers, his hips rocking in a slow rhythm that built in small increments that had her clawing at his back and digging her heels into his thighs in an attempt to make him move faster. He chuckled into her mouth and kept up his torturous pace.

Cassie groaned. Her pussy convulsed with the desperate need for more and she pulled her mouth free of his to trail her lips over his shoulder. She scraped his skin with her teeth, pulled him closer with her arms and legs and drove her hips up to meet his every thrust.

"Move, dammit." Cassie dug her nails into him.

"You want faster?" he spoke into her hair.

"Yes." There was no hiding the raw edge of need in her voice.

He slowed down further. "You don't like slow?"

"No."

He angled his hips and the base of his shaft hit her swollen clit.

"Yes."

"Make up your mind." She could hear the smile in his voice.

"Fast," Cassie panted. "Faster. Harder."

"Harder?" Lucas drove his length into her in a bone-jarring slam that had her pussy clenching and her vision blurring. "Is that what you mean?"

"God. Yes." Her nails stabbed into him as she clung to his back. "Yes."

She was so close. Her muscles were coiled tight and ready to let go in what would no doubt be a blinding orgasm. He picked up the pace. Advance and retreat, over and over, as they raced for the top together.

"C'mon, Cass." Lucas pushed up on his elbows until his torso was suspended above hers, the part of their bodies slamming together visible to both of them when they looked down. "Fuck, that's hot."

Cassie had to agree. His condom-covered cock glistened with her juices and her nether lips flared out around his shaft as he withdrew. She'd never seen anything as sexy or done anything this raunchy. He'd shown her a new kind of sex—a new side of herself. And as she gazed down at his cock impaling her time after time, she let go. Shattered into a thousand million pieces.

"Luc."

Lucas followed her, his body ramming into hers one final time before he held still, shuddering with release. "Cass."

He collapsed to the side, half-on and half-off her, their bodies still joined intimately, and Cassie wondered how she was ever going to walk away from this man and all he made her feel.

14

"Oy, Cassie, wait up!"

Cassie turned to find West jogging across the car park. "Hey, West, what's up?" She waited for him to catch up.

"I need to run the weekend's comings and goings by you."

"Why? You have a key. You come and go as you need. Just label everything clearly for my staff." West walked beside her.

"Don't I always?" He grabbed the door and pulled it open, ushering her through before him. "Actually, I wanted to check it was okay to use the kitchen for personal use."

She glanced his way. "Personal? Sure, you paid for the thing, use it however you want."

"Thanks."

"So, what's the personal thing or is it a secret?"

"Not a secret, but…" West ducked his head, but not before Cassie saw his cheeks flush red.

"Oh my God! Are you blushing?"

He grabbed her in a headlock before she could rib him anymore. "Knock it off, squirt."

Cassie laughed. "Big bad Weston Mann has a crush," she sing-songed.

"I'm warning you." West rubbed his knuckles on the top of her head while tightening his grip and bringing her head closer to his chest. He smelled like the yummy curry puffs that were one of his company's specialties.

"You don't sca—"

Cassie was ripped from West's arms as Luc's voice boomed through the warehouse. "Get your hands off her!"

"Whoa!"

Cassie peeked around Lucas to see West with his hands up as though a gun was pointed at him. She had to check there wasn't one in Luc's hand. Just in case. Although with the way Lucas vibrated with tension he probably didn't need a gun to kill West. If she didn't step in quickly this could turn into a bloodbath she wasn't in the mood to deal with. Not today.

"Lucas, we were just mucking around." Cassie tried to step between them but Luc put his arm out and stopped her.

"He had you in a headlock," he growled.

"Yes, but he wasn't hurting me, and it's not the first time he's done it. Probably won't be the last either." Cassie rolled her eyes behind his back.

"Yes. It will." Luc's tone brokered no argument, and with West still standing there with his hands in the air he obviously wasn't going to give one.

"Seriously?" Cassie shoved at Luc's back. "Who the fuck do you think you are?" She thumped his back with her fists.

"What?" He spun around and grabbed her wrists to stop her from hitting him again. "Why are you beating me up?"

She glared at him. "Because you're acting like a Neanderthal idiot, that's why!" Cassie yelled.

"I wasn't the one with my arm around your neck!" Luc yelled back.

"He wasn't trying to hurt me, you moron." Cassie couldn't believe anyone could think West would actually hurt her. She turned to West, but before she could say anything West took a step back.

"I'll go get started on those pastries you need done today." West turned, but Cassie reached out and grabbed his shirt.

"No, you don't. You're not getting away that easily." She yanked on his shirt. "Turn around so I can introduce you two so next time Luc doesn't rip your damn head off."

West reluctantly turned around. "Fine." He crossed his arms over his chest.

"Lucas Wilhelm, meet Weston Mann, better known as West. West, Luc." She waved her hand between the two of them. "Now, if we're finished playing damsel in distress, bodyguard and villain, I have work to do."

Cassie didn't wait for either of them to say a word. She spun on her heel and headed for the stairs. Taking them two at a time, she mumbled about idiot men until she reached her office where she took great pleasure in slamming her door.

The air slid from her lungs when she saw the neatly wrapped present sitting in the center of her desk. Cautiously, she made her way across the room and picked up the small box. A tiny card attached read:

Cassie,

These remind me of your eyes.

Luc

With shaking fingers, Cassie tore open the pretty paper to find a silver box. Lifting the lid, she stared at the glass bead bracelet inside. The beads were a selection of browns and golds. Her breath stalled. Luc must have made it at the birthday party on the weekend.

It was such an unexpected gesture. One that pulled at every conviction she had that she shouldn't see him anymore. She fell into her chair, the leather creaking beneath her, and contemplated what it meant. He'd let her walk out the door this morning without a word about seeing her again. And now he was leaving her a gift.

Cassie closed her eyes and dropped her head back. Just when she thought she was okay with her decision to cool things with Luc, he went and did something that threw up a host of unwanted emotions.

The biggest being longing. How could she want a man so deeply when she'd only known him three days?

Her phone rang, snapping her out of her thoughts. She didn't have time to dwell on her personal life, she had a business to run, and that was exactly why she shouldn't see him. Lucas was too much of a distraction and Cassie couldn't afford that any more than she could a Ferrari.

∼

LUC WATCHED Cassie until she disappeared from sight. He guessed he owed her and this guy, West, an apology. He'd fucked up. She couldn't blame him though. Seeing her caught in a headlock just about exploded *his* head.

Every instinct in him had gone on red alert at the scene he'd found when he'd come down the stairs five minutes ago. Having never laid eyes on West before, Luc's first impulse was to think threat, especially when the guy had Cassie in such a menacing hold.

"Cassie hasn't mentioned you, so I assume you're someone she just met."

He turned to find West had stepped closer. The guy had puffed out his chest and stood ramrod straight too. Probably in an attempt to intimidate him, but Luc didn't scare easily, so the guy was shit out of luck. "Yeah." Luc wasn't about to reveal anything about him and Cassie.

West grinned. "The strong, silent type, are you?"

The mockery in the guy's voice set Luc's nerves on edge, not that they weren't already there. "If Cassie wants to tell you anything that's up to her, but I'm not about to share my business with you." Luc turned to leave but West's next words stopped him.

"Want to know how to win her over?"

He turned back to face a smirking West.

"Yeah, thought you might, but let me give you some info first." West crossed his arms and squared his shoulders. "I've known Cassie since I was a kid. Her brother is my best friend and I've been to as many family events at the Moreland house as she has, so I know a little more about the woman than most."

Luc's gut churned. He didn't like that West had so much history with Cassie. Didn't like the implied intimacy of it. He opened his mouth but stopped when West held up a hand.

"No. I've never gone there. Never thought of going there, so don't insult us both by asking. She's always been a kid sister to me regardless of our lack of blood ties." West stepped forward and got in Luc's face. He had to give the guy credit. He had balls. Luc topped him by a good three inches. "You fuck her over and it's not just me you'll deal with. She's got five older brothers who would gladly take you apart with me."

Luc laughed. He couldn't help it. And when West scowled at him, he laughed harder.

"Listen—"

"Sorry, not laughing at you." Luc sucked in a breath and got his mirth under control. "I just find it hilarious that you even think there'd be anything left if I fucked her over. She doesn't need you or her brothers to fight her battles. She'd have me castrated, drawn and quartered and hung from the nearest lamppost before I ever *fucked her over*."

West smiled. "Ah, so you have met the real Cassie then."

"Oh, yeah. We spent most of Friday night butting heads."

"Obviously something changed between now and then, though."

Ah, they were back to fishing for info. "Something changes every second."

"You know, I think I like you." West stuck out his hand. "West Mann."

Luc gripped his hand and shook. "Luc Wilhelm."

"So, about winning her over."

"At this point." He turned his head to look over at the stairs Cassie had disappeared up. "I'll take any advice you have."

"Don't push her. Let her come to you, but don't let her think you're not hanging around. Small things will get her over the big ones, so don't go ordering flowers or some such shit. Stick with simple things like making sure she's got lunch on a busy day. She's always forgetting to eat and then she'll gorge on chocolate bars or those horrible TV dinners she has in her freezer." West shuddered as he said the last part.

Luc could see how that might work. And he wanted to look after her, wanted to be sure she took care of herself. She'd already admitted to eating crap most of the time. "Thanks. I'll keep that in mind."

"No worries. Just don't go overboard. Something simple will get her every time. She's a sucker for thoughtful gestures, not so much the extravagant ones like jewelry."

Jewelry. *Shit.* He hoped she wouldn't think the bracelet was over the top. It was only a kids' party trinket not a diamond ring. He looked toward the stairs again. She hadn't come back down and thrown it at him. And surely she'd found and opened it by now.

Then again, maybe she'd tossed it in the bin. Luc hoped not, but he didn't really have a say now that he'd given it to her. She'd do with it whatever she wanted. He'd just have to accept any choice she made.

West's hand clapped him on the shoulder. "Good luck, man."

Luc turned back to him. "Thanks." He smiled but he wasn't really feeling it. For the first time since Cassie had walked out his door this morning, he had real concern about the outcome of their relationship.

CASSIE LOOKED up from her paperwork at Dan. "Thanks, but I don't recall you asking me if I wanted anything for lunch."

"You didn't." He put the paper bag on her desk. "And I didn't order it."

Before she could get a word out, he'd turned to leave.

"Wait. What do you mean you didn't order it?" she called to his retreating back.

"The deli down the street delivered it," he said over his shoulder.

Cassie stared at the bag. He hadn't. Not again. It was the same yesterday. And the day before. And both nights. Lunch and dinner, Monday, Tuesday and now Wednesday. She didn't see him during the day, but he was always either waiting—with food—in his car, or on her doorstep within seconds of her getting home. He'd not stayed. Instead, he'd delivered her meals and left. That confused her more than anything.

Why would he not want to stick around and eat with her?

Confused and frustrated, she reached for the bag and ripped it open. A BLT. Her mouth watered.

Damn, he'd ordered her favourite sandwich.

She sighed. It was even toasted.

How was she supposed to keep her distance when he kept doing nice things for her? The man was making it hard to stand by her decision not to continue their all-consuming relationship. Plus he was making her arguments about distractions useless when he wasn't around during the day to interrupt her work and barely said ten words to her at night.

She peeled back the wrapper and sank her teeth into the sandwich, closing her eyes as salty bacon flavor flooded her mouth. She polished off half before putting it down. Cassie grabbed her phone and she flicked through her address book until she came to Luc's number.

She'd programmed it in after asking Jody for it. It'd felt strange to have to ask her new employee for a number she should already have, but Jody hadn't seemed fazed by the request and rattled it off without a second thought.

Thumb hovering over the screen, she debated calling him or texting. She wasn't sure how she'd react to hearing his voice, so she pulled up a new message and fired off a quick thank you. Within seconds her phone beeped with a reply.

You're welcome.

Cassie tapped out a reply. *You can't keep doing this.*

Again his reply fired back. *Why not?*

Yes, why not? It was a good question and Cassie couldn't think of a good answer. It took her a few minutes to think of a reason, but even then she knew it wasn't a strong argument. *Because you can't keep paying for my food.*

You can pay next week.

Cassie laughed. The man was insane.

And not going away.

But she had to be honest.

As much as she didn't want to see him again, she did. If she found him on her doorstep tonight she'd invite him in before he could run off. She'd been too shocked to think the last two nights so he'd gotten away with little more than a nod hello from her.

That changed today. She fingered the beads around her wrist. He hadn't said anything to her about the bracelet. Not yet, but she knew he'd seen her wearing it Monday night.

She wasn't sure why she'd put it on. With everything she'd told herself about not getting attached to him, even she couldn't understand why she wanted to wear it. Okay, that was a lie. If she was going to start lying to herself she was in trouble.

She'd put it on and kept it on because Luc had made it. For her. It was a way to keep him close without keeping him close, and wasn't that just fucked-up reasoning. Cassie let out a deep breath and slouched back in her chair. Her phone beeped, bouncing on the desk as it vibrated with an incoming message.

Is it yummy? Mine is.

A smile curved her mouth. They were having lunch together. *Yes.*

How does pizza for dinner sound?

Will you join me?

Can't.

Cassie frowned and sent a text with a frowny face in reply.

Have to work but I'll order the pizza for 7. Sound good?

She didn't want to eat alone again and really she should just organize her own dinner. *Don't worry, I'll take care of myself tonight.*

Too late. Ordered already.

Damn him. *Fine. But I'm cooking tomorrow night.*

Aren't you working tomorrow night?

Shit. She was. Wait. How did he know that? *How do you know?*

Jody mentioned it.

Plausible. He'd obviously been speaking to his sister, and Cassie knew he was worried about Jody, so she fired off a quick message to alleviate some of his concern.

She's doing great. She'll be running her own events in no time. Thanks for sending her my way.

You're both welcome. Gotta go. Meeting. See you later.

Cassie read his last message over and over. Did he mean he'd see her tonight? He'd said he'd ordered her a pizza but he wouldn't be there, so was he planning on stopping by after he finished work? A pang of disappointment and a bubble of hope vied for space in her chest. She'd see-sawed back and forth about what she wanted so often over the last few days that she was beginning to get motion sickness.

She leaned forward and thunked her head on the desk. There was no getting around it. Lucas Wilhelm wasn't just a distraction. He was a roadblock.

15

Cassie stared at the man on her doorstep. It was Thursday evening and the fourth day in a row she'd seen or heard from him. Monday morning, when she'd left his house determined not to think about him and all he'd made her feel in one weekend, she'd thought that was the end of it.

She'd been wrong. Lucas had been in her face but not.

He'd found an excuse every day since then to see her. She wanted to be pissed off about it, only the thrill of excitement that swept through her with each sighting wouldn't let her get a good mad up. Besides, he never stayed for long and *that* was beginning to piss her off. He was teasing her with his presence only to disappear before she could give in to her body's desire for his.

She sighed. Damn the man. She got out of her car and then took her time shutting the door to gather her thoughts before she walked toward him. He pushed off the wall and picked up the plastic bags at his feet.

The closer she got, the more obvious it became that he'd brought dinner. Again. He'd fed her lunch and dinner every day this week. Cassie suspected he was getting her work schedule from his sister, Jody, because he seemed to know exactly where she'd be at all times.

It was Jody who'd insisted she head home now. Insisted she and Dan had tonight's cocktail party under control. And Luc had even mentioned she was working tonight, so he had to have known she was heading home early somehow.

The mouthwatering aroma of curry wafted toward her and all turbulent thoughts stopped. "Oh my God, is that Indian?" She stepped onto her small porch.

"Yep. Complete with naan bread." Lucas raised the bags and shook them slightly.

Shit. She couldn't turn him away now even if she wanted to. Not when he'd brought her favourite food and her stomach was rumbling with hunger. Slipping her key in the lock, she twisted and glanced over at him. "Is that for one or two?"

"Two?" He arched one thick brow.

Well, this was a first. He was planning to eat with her this time. Cassie shoved the door open.

"Come in. If you want to put all that in the kitchen I'm just going to get out of these work clothes first, then I'll dish it up." She headed down the hall to her room, the sound of Lucas shutting the door and moving toward the kitchen behind her.

A smile curled her lips and Cassie had to admit, if only to herself, that she was pleased he was here. With each quick visit she'd missed him more. She couldn't count the number of times her mind had wandered to thoughts of Lucas over the last few days.

He'd found his way deeper than just under her skin, and as much as she'd told herself she didn't have time for a relationship, she couldn't fight the needs rising inside her. And it wasn't only about the sex either. As good as it was between them physically, there was an emotional connection too.

It was time she faced facts and accepted the feelings he provoked and dealt with them. And him. She stripped out of her work clothes and grabbed a T-shirt and shorts. Stepping into the pants, she thought about how the next few hours might go.

If his constant appearance in her life was a clue, then she could only conclude that he wanted to move past their weekend together into a possible future. The very idea of spending more time with Luc heated her blood and sent a shiver down her spine.

She'd been fooling herself. She couldn't deny their connection, and her arguments against seeing him held no real substance when he'd not once interfered with her work schedule.

Her last venture into relationship territory had blown up in her face when her ex had turned up to a job she was overseeing one Saturday afternoon. He'd caused a huge scene, and she'd been forced to refund the client's money. Not to mention word had gotten around and she'd lost three more bookings because of his angry outburst.

Cassie had to admit that she'd been gun shy with men since, and she'd been unfair to Lucas by assuming he'd behave the same as her ex and using it as an excuse to keep her distance. Shame washed through her.

She owed Luc an apology and an explanation. He deserved both whether he wanted to continue seeing her or not. She'd take his frequent visits as a good sign and hope her fear of getting involved hadn't ruined any possible future for them.

With what had to be a goofy smile on her face, Cassie tugged her top on and headed out of her room to find Lucas. She found him in her dining room, table set with two places and the food spread out in front of them. Watching him as he poured them both a glass of water, she felt warm and soft.

It would be easy to get used to seeing him there. Too easy perhaps, but she wasn't going to dwell on that. Instead, she'd make the most of enjoying a meal with a great guy and see where things went.

Luc leaned back in his chair and rubbed his stomach. Dan had been right. The little Indian place in Balgowlah made *the* best Indian food outside of India. It also happened to be Cassie's favourite take-away dinner. He'd eaten more than he should, but the flavors had been too mouthwatering to give up.

Cassie was still going. She'd probably eaten as much as if not more than him already, but that didn't stop her from scooping up another spoonful of Baltic curry.

"Good?" he asked even though he knew the answer already.

"Mmm…" She swallowed. "Delicious."

She slipped her tongue out and licked across her bottom lip. Luc's groin tightened. Dinner had been a study in restraint and he was beginning to think he might not be able to stick to his plan of hands off for much longer. Dragging in a deep breath, he reined in his libido and tried to distract himself with mundane chatter.

"So Jody's working out?" Discussing his sister was bound to dampen his arousal.

"Yes." Cassie wiped her mouth with a napkin. "Like I said yesterday, she's great. She and Dan have had a few hiccups, but I think that's because he's still against bringing in another supervisor."

"Really?" Luc had been speaking with Dan all week. The guy didn't seem the type to hold a grudge against someone who wasn't at fault, and Jody definitely had nothing to do with Cassie expanding her management base.

Cassie's forehead wrinkled. "Actually, I'm not sure if it is that. There's some crazy sparks flying off those two."

Sparks? As in sexual sparks? *Shit.* Luc needed to call his sister. The last thing she needed was another man fucking up her life.

"Whatever it is, they don't let it interfere with the job and that's all that matters." She waved her hand in the air. "But enough about work. I'm home early for the first time in months. I want to enjoy it while I can."

"Okay, how about we watch some TV?"

She glanced at her watch. "You know I wouldn't have a clue what's on at this time anymore. I can't remember the last time I sat in front of a TV and vegged out."

Luc laughed. "That would be last weekend when we watched *An American President.*"

Cassie's cheeks turned a pretty shade of pink. "Yeah, well, I didn't exactly watch it."

"No, but you certainly vegged out." He pushed his chair back and stood. "I'll clear this away, you go see if there's anything on."

"Don't be silly. You made dinner, I'll clean up."

"I didn't make it."

"Still, you organized it, so I'm on cleanup duty." She stacked the empty containers on top of their plates and carried them to the kitchen. "Do you want a coffee or something?" she called out.

"No. I'm good." Luc wandered into her living room and picked up the remote from the side table. He flicked through channels before he found an episode of *The Big Bang Theory*. "You okay with a comedy?"

"Sure." She came into the room carrying a tray with a plate of Tim Tams and two glasses of water. "Snacks." She grinned.

"Snacks? We just finished dinner. I couldn't possibly eat another thing." Luc dropped to the couch behind him.

"There's always room for Tim Tams." Cassie set the tray down on the coffee table and sat beside him. "But I'll happily eat your share."

He smiled. "I just bet you will."

Relaxing back, Luc pretended to focus on the TV when every cell in his body was tuned to the woman next to him. He didn't want to push her, but damn, he really, really wanted to get his hands on her again.

The no-pressure, take-their-time course was wearing thin, and he couldn't tell if his slow wooing of Cassie had gotten him any closer to the goal. He'd give anything to be able to read her mind, and while he'd wanted to pump his sister and Dan for information, he hadn't. Now he wished he'd given in and asked either of them if she'd at least mentioned him.

"You're thinking too hard." Her words jolted him out of his thoughts.

"What?"

"You accused me of overthinking last weekend." She turned on the seat next to him, her knee pressing into his thigh. "And you were right. I was worrying this thing between us to death. Now you're doing it."

One side of his mouth kicked up. "Yeah, I am."

"I need to explain something."

Luc sat up straighter, her tone sending a shaft of dread through him. "Go ahead."

"I had a bad experience with my last boyfriend. We dated for a few months and when all my time was taken up by establishing Are You Game?, he made it clear he wasn't happy. He wanted me to spend more time with him, and when I wouldn't cut back my hours, he turned up at a child's birthday party and made such a scene that I not only had to refund the client's money, I lost bookings too."

"Asshole." Luc wanted to find the guy and punch him.

Cassie laughed. "Yeah, turned out he was."

A thought occurred to him. "How long ago was this?"

"Two years."

"And you haven't dated since then?" Luc wasn't sure if he was pleased by her lack of dating or upset that some jerk had hurt her so badly that she'd erected walls around herself.

"No, you're the first guy I've even looked at, never mind spent time with."

He grinned, pleased to have been the one to break through her shell. "Do you think I'm going to do what that asshole did? Demand more time than you have?"

"No. Yes. No." She sighed. "It was a knee-jerk reaction. I'd have been the same with anyone."

"But I'm not just anyone, Cass."

Luc watched her throat work as she swallowed. Watched her tongue slip out to slide across her lip before she spoke. "No. You're not."

"Who am I?" He waited to see if she remembered what he'd said nearly a week ago.

"You're the guy who's going to bring me to my knees."

He smiled. "Yeah, but want to know something?"

"What?"

"I'm going to be right there beside you. On my knees, holding your hand."

Her eyes widened, her lips parting a fraction as she sucked in a breath. "Y-you are?"

"I'm already there, Cass, just waiting for you to join me."

"Oh."

Luc waited for her to say more, but she didn't. His stomach dropped like a lead ball. He couldn't take back what he'd said or the depth of his feelings the words revealed, but he could make it easier for her. "Wanna catch a movie with me sometime this weekend?"

She smiled. "I'd like that."

"Good. Let me know what time suits you. I'm free all weekend." He didn't want to push her and send her running for the hills, so he'd take whatever he could get when he could get it. That might make him desperate, but he didn't care. When it came to Cassie, he felt desperate.

Cassie reached over and smoothed the skin between his eyebrows. "You're doing it again."

"What?"

"Overthinking."

He shrugged. "Maybe."

"Want to know what I think?" She didn't give him time to answer. "I think we should just go with it. See each other when we can. Let's not label it or stress about where it's going. We'll enjoy it while it lasts. No strings."

"I've got one string." He leaned toward her.

"Oh yeah, what?" Her breath fanned over his face.

"We're exclusive."

Cassie reared back. "Of course. Jeez, I barely have time to see you. How the hell would I fit in anyone else?"

He stuck out his hand. "So we have a deal?"

She looked at his hand then brought her gaze back to his. "Oh, I think we can seal the deal better than that."

Before he could register the words, Cassie was in his arms and her mouth was on his. Once his brain unfroze, he took what he'd been craving all week. He thrust his tongue between her teeth and coaxed hers out.

Slipping his hands under her T-shirt, Luc found her breasts and made quick work of flicking the front closure of her bra undone. Her soft mounds fell into his hands, her nipples growing hard against his palms. With thumb and forefinger, he tweaked the tips until they were puckered tight.

"God, yes. Do that again," she breathed into his mouth, and Luc obliged.

He played with her breasts while taking her mouth in a soul-deep kiss. It wasn't long before neither of them was satisfied with just kissing. She pulled free and grabbed the hem of her top. Whipping it up and over her head, her voice was muffled but the demand was clear.

"Clothes. Off. Now."

Luc didn't want to take Cassie on her couch this first time. He wanted to lay her out and reacquaint himself with every inch of her. "Bedroom."

He scooped her up as he stood. She slipped her arms around his neck and her legs wrapped around his waist. His blood pounded in his ears as he made his way down the hall to her room. Using his foot, Luc pushed the door open and strode to the bed where he fell forward. Bracing his elbows, he took his weight on his arms while pinning her beneath him.

"I want you naked and spread out before me," he growled in her ear, his arousal already at a fever pitch.

She wiggled against him. "Then you better let me up so I can get naked."

Luc didn't need to be told twice. He sprang to his feet and began tugging off his clothes as he watched Cassie do the same. Damn, she was sexy. She wasn't even trying to turn him on and she had him panting and drooling.

This wasn't going to last long. Not the first time at least. He'd beaten her by a pair of undies, but they were the sexiest strip of pink lace he'd ever seen so he didn't care that she wasn't naked yet. Grinning, he launched himself back on top of her as she kicked her undies off.

He swallowed her gasp as he took her mouth with his. They

rubbed against each other, both seeking the friction necessary to find release. Luc shoved his knee between hers and spread her legs wide. Her hips cradled his, her pussy the perfect resting place for his throbbing cock. She was hot and wet and he couldn't wait another second to be inside her.

"I need to be inside. Now."

"Condoms are in the drawer." She tilted her head to the left.

Scrambling over her, Luc retrieved the unopened box of condoms. He tore the plastic off and grabbed a foil packet, ripping it open in record time.

"Here. Let me." Cassie took the protection from him and began to sheath his length.

Luc clenched his jaw, gritted his teeth and tried to think of something other than Cassie's hands on his cock. It was such a close thing that the second the protection was in place he pushed her to her back and jumped on top. All finesse deserted him in his driving need to be buried within her tight depths. She spread her legs and welcomed him with outstretched arms. Taking her invitation, he thrust into her.

A cry tore from her throat. The sound, one of shocked pleasure, sent a bolt of lust through his veins. He couldn't hold back. She was like a drug he'd been withdrawing from all week, and now that he'd had a dose he couldn't stop. Hard and fast, he surged in and out. Her back bowed, her hips rising to meet his with each plunge. They rocked together in a rapid tempo that pushed them both over the edge in minutes.

Cassie cried out, "Luc."

Her pussy walls clenched around his cock in a red-hot grip that bathed his entire length in fire and lit the fuse in his balls. His orgasm slammed into him. Come bursting free like a bullet from a gun. And the recoil was just as bad. He shuddered and trembled as he continued to empty himself. Air sawed in and out of his heaving chest and he collapsed forward, unable to do more than bend his elbows and hope he wasn't crushing her.

"Jesus, I think you killed me."

He smiled against her throat. "My sentiments exactly."

She laughed, her breasts vibrating where they were pressed into his chest. "But what a way to go, right?"

Luc couldn't find the energy to speak again, so he nodded. He needed a second to catch his breath and then he'd move. For now he was more than happy to stay spread over Cassie with his still-hard cock buried in her sweet pussy.

"I think we should do that again. Make sure it wasn't a fluke."

"No fluke. Just Cassie."

"Oh no, I'm not taking all the credit for that." She ran her hand up his spine and into the hair at his nape. "If it was just me, I'd have been this blissed out before now. It's the two of us together."

"Then we better stay together. Besides, after that you've ruined me for all other women. You better take pity on me and let me stick around."

Cassie laughed. "Ditto, buddy." She slapped his ass. "Now get off me. The fact I can't breathe is beginning to annoy me."

Luc levered himself up and to the side. His cock slid from her body and both of them shuddered in reaction. He slid his hand under his belly and removed the used condom. He still hadn't gone down, but there was nothing he could do about it until he regained some of his strength. Cassie had wiped him out. A glance to the side showed her sprawled on her back, one arm thrown over her head. She looked as done in as he felt.

At least his quick draw and fire hadn't left her wanting.

A smile curled his mouth and he closed his eyes. He couldn't help thinking about what he and Cassie had. They had chemistry in spades, but it was the friendship and admiration that was growing between them that had him thinking of the future she told him not to worry about.

No matter how much he argued against it being too soon, he knew Cassie was in his life to stay. She was everything he'd ever wanted without knowing it.

"Cass?" He opened his eyes to look at her.

"Hmm."

"This is going to get complicated, you know that, right?"

She sighed and turned her head toward him. "Yeah, I know."

"And you're okay with that?" Luc didn't want to pressure her but he needed her to know where he was in this.

"Surprisingly, yes." She reached over and brushed her fingertips down his cheek. "Last week I would have said no. Four days ago I would have said no, but I can't argue with this. Nor do I want to."

"We'll go as slow as you need."

Cassie smiled. "Thank you. Although I'm a little offended that you think I'm the one who'll need time."

Luc grabbed her wrist and brought her hand to his mouth, placing a kiss in the center of her palm. "You don't want to know how fast I want to take this."

"Tell me." She grinned. "Not that I'll agree to your pace."

"Move in with me."

"Shit! Yeah, not happening anytime soon."

"Let me have a drawer in your dresser, clothes hanging in your wardrobe, a toothbrush in your bathroom."

"We can probably work our way up to those in the next few weeks."

Luc sat up quickly. "Really? You're okay with sleepovers? With personal space being encroached?"

Her forehead wrinkled. "I think so."

"Promise you'll tell me if I push too fast or something I do freaks you out." He leaned over her and brought his mouth within a breath of hers. "Promise me."

"I promise."

"We need to seal the deal." Luc smiled as he took Cassie's mouth with his. Long moments later, he pulled his mouth from hers and stared at her.

"What?" She licked her lips and Luc's gaze immediately returned to her kiss-swollen mouth.

"You."

"What about me?"

"You're here."

She shoved at his chest. "Don't get all mushy on me, Lucas."

"Sorry. I can't help it. You fill me with something I've never had before."

"What?"

"I can't explain it, but I can show you." He rocked his hips against her, his erection trapped between them.

"I think you have it backward. It's not me filling you." She laughed.

Luc chuckled. "Then let me fill you."

EPILOGUE

Cassie scanned the room and found nothing out of place. Jody had done a great job on her first event. She really did need to thank Luc for suggesting his sister for the new supervisor's position. The party was well into the second hour and was already a success.

Music thumped through the house's sound system, food made the rounds on silver trays held by black-tuxedo-wearing wait staff and glasses were turned bottoms up quicker than they could be filled. Sydney's social elite were letting their hair—and pants—down. Heading in the direction of the pants-dropper, Cassie was beaten there by Dan.

He'd insisted on attending tonight's event along with her even though it was Jody's job. There was tension between her new and old employees that she needed to keep an eye on. Cassie had known Dan was against hiring new staff, but she didn't think he would carry his anger this far.

Fortunately, Jody either didn't notice Dan's open hostility, or she was choosing to ignore it—and him. Smiling, she watched Jody enter the room and quickly extricate the unclothed guest from Dan and remove him from the room. She chuckled at the consternation on Dan's face.

"What's so funny?" Warm breath fanned over her ear and neck, and the unmistakable scent of Luc surrounded her.

Smiling, she turned around and looked up. "Luc. What are you doing here?"

He leaned down and placed a hard peck on her lips. "Can't seem to stay away from my woman."

She frowned. "We've talked about that."

"Aw, c'mon, Cass." Luc scowled at her. "We've been seeing each other exclusively for four months, don't you think it's about time you accepted that you're mine and I'm yours?"

Her stomach flipped. He'd been so patient with her, letting her dictate how much they saw each other and where. She knew he was getting frustrated with her inability to commit to more than casual dating and hot sex. And it was super-hot sex.

They couldn't keep their hands off each other. Which was why she wasn't ready to take their relationship to the next level. Only a few people knew they were an item. Someone bumped into her back and she was abruptly reminded of their surroundings.

"We can't have this discussion here," she said.

"Fine." Luc grabbed her hand and wove his fingers through hers. He all but yanked her off her feet as he spun around and began pushing his way through the crowd.

She stumbled in her attempt to keep up and he slid his arm around her waist and clamped her to his side. They hit the hallway where the crowd thinned out, but she needn't have worried about someone overhearing the rest of their conversation.

Before she could gasp a breath, Luc opened a door, shoved her inside a closet and followed. Darkness enveloped her and she threw her hands out to protect herself from crashing into the wall.

"Jesus, Luc, what the fuck?"

He spun her around, and with his hands on her ribs, lifted her off the floor. "Put your legs around me," he demanded.

His mouth found hers before she moved. For a split second, she froze. Then everything moved at once. Her blood rushed, her heart slammed against her sternum and her arms and legs wrapped around him. He drove his tongue between her lips and stroked hers with wicked intent.

Like all their kisses, it shot to carnal desperation in a heartbeat. This was why she couldn't hand herself over to him completely. This desperate, clawing need that took her under within a breath had her careening out of control faster than a speeding car and wiped her mind clear of all except Luc.

She dug her fingers into his scalp and pulled him closer. He nipped at her lips, trailed his mouth over her cheek to her ear where he set about driving her insane. Licking and nibbling at the delicate flesh, he had her panting for breath and begging for more.

"Oh, God, Luc. Please."

"You can't deny me, Cass," he growled against her skin.

She couldn't. As much as she wanted to, wanted to protect her heart from the pain he could inflict, she accepted that it was already too late. He'd stormed her defenses and left her bare.

He buried his face in her neck and breathed deep. "Dammit. Cass." Her name was a plea and she tightened her body around him in reflex—in comfort.

"Luc." She kissed his head and held on while he continued to crush her against him.

"I need you." He rocked his hips and pressed his hard cock into her sex.

"Yes."

Luc did it again and Cassie all but purred as sensation fired through her pussy.

They wasted no time in ridding themselves of their clothes. In the months since they first had sex, they'd perfected the art of removing the minimum necessary to get what they needed.

He set her down and her nimble fingers quickly worked the button and zip on his pants before shoving them down his thighs. She sucked in a breath. Commando. The knowledge that he'd been naked beneath his jeans speared through her. She reached out to wrap her hand around his thick shaft.

Luc pushed her skirt up over her hips. He curled his fingers into the sides of her panties and yanked them down her legs as he dropped to his knees before her. He buried his face in her pussy, thrusting his tongue out to probe between her folds.

The first flick on her clit made her gasp. The second made her tremble. The third had her collapsing to the floor. With his help, she slid onto his lap.

"Take me inside," he murmured against her mouth.

Reaching between them, Cassie raised her hips and, hand around his length, guided him home. She sank down and took him in. The angle drove him deep and they moaned in unison when her body sat flush to his.

"Fuck, I'm glad you went on the pill." Luc wrapped his hand in her ponytail and tugged her head back so he could meet her gaze. "This is the best damn place in the world. You're the best damn thing in the world."

She smiled at his words. He always took their coupling, no matter how raw and dirty, to an emotional level. Without fail, he took more than her body every time. A lump formed in her throat, her mouth dry as she struggled to see his eyes and all they could reveal in the darkness.

"Ride me, Cass. Show me heaven, baby."

He gripped her hips and helped her find a rhythm. Up and down, she took him in, let him out. Long glides of slick swollen flesh over rigid steel. He bucked up as she plunged down, driving them quickly to the edge. They picked up the pace as they moved closer to release.

Her clit slammed into the base of his cock each time he hit bottom and she found his mouth with hers, wanting to taste him as she went over.

Luc growled into her mouth as the first spasm gripped her. The walls of her pussy convulsed around him, sucking him deeper as he took control and drove himself up into her with savage thrusts.

Light exploded behind her eyelids as she came apart completely.

Seconds later, Luc followed, setting off another set of rolling contractions in her core. Their mouths separated as they gasped for air.

She curled into him, sought the closeness she only ever found with Luc. He held her, rubbed his hands up and down her back as they came down from another mind-blowing encounter. "How can it keep getting better?" she mumbled into his shoulder.

"You know why." He kissed her temple. "I can't hold it in any longer, Cass. I know you're not ready to hear what I have to say, but I'm not expecting anything more than you're willing to give. Shit. I'll take any scrap you'll throw my way."

Cassie leaned back to look at him. The darkness was no longer blinding, her eyes having adjusted to the lack of light, but she still couldn't quite make out the expression on his face. She didn't want to believe what she thought she saw for fear it was a trick her heart was playing on her.

Luc trailed a finger along her lips. "I love you, Cass."

She jerked, fear and longing warring inside her. "I...I..."

He placed his finger over her mouth. "Shh. Don't say anything. I don't need to hear it back, Cass, but I need you to hear it. Need you to let me love you."

"Oh, Luc." Cassie threw her arms around him and hugged him close. "I love you too."

Luc's whole body sighed in relief. He'd been holding back for weeks —months—and he'd finally decided that hell would probably freeze over before Cassie declared her love first. He understood her reluctance. They were so out of control when it came to being together. Neither of them could keep their hands to themselves for long.

Tonight was a classic example. His intention had been to find her and help out before taking her home to bed where he'd reveal his love for her in a romantic setting. Instead, he'd taken her in a closet.

He rolled his eyes and held her tighter. She'd been a breath of fresh air in his life these last few months, and he knew to his marrow that he couldn't live without her. He'd hoped she'd come around, but as the days ticked by with her still keeping him at a distance, he'd realized he'd have to push her, nudge her in the right direction.

It was probably underhanded, and some of what he had planned to convince her a trip down the aisle was required was definitely sneaky, but the end was worth it. Everything about Cassie was worth it.

They'd taken the first step. Now he just had to keep them moving in the right direction. She squirmed against him and Luc's softened cock pulsed with renewed lust. It never failed to amaze him that he could want her so badly after just having had her. But there was no denying the driving need that consumed him where Cassie was concerned.

He dropped a kiss on her cheek and then gripped her waist and lifted her off his lap. Her cry broke the silence and a matching moan rumbled in his chest. His balls throbbed and blood filled his length once more.

On wobbly legs, Cassie stood in front of him. Luc climbed to his feet and reached behind to feel the wall for a light switch. There was no way he was searching for their clothes in the dark. Both of them blinked when the room lit up.

Squinting, Luc looked down and found Cassie's underwear. He helped her step into them before scooping up his jeans and thrusting one leg into them. Hopping on one foot, he slid the second leg in while she straightened her skirt. They didn't say a word.

Worried, he tipped up her chin so she'd look at him. "You okay?"

The smile she gifted him warmed his heart. "Are you kidding? Not only did the man I love just declare his love for me, but I got to play seven minutes in heaven with him."

Luc laughed. "Seven minutes in heaven with you is nowhere near enough." He leaned down and kissed her.

"Mmm...you're right. We should get out of here." She spoke against his lips. "I think Jody has it under control, so how 'bout we head home for another slice of heaven?"

"Lead the way." He stepped aside and swept his arm out to let her go first.

Cassie opened the door and strode into the hall like it was perfectly normal to be leaving the hall closet with a guy you'd just fucked senseless. He'd barely shut the door after them when a blonde with silicone breasts, trowelled on make-up and an outfit no bigger than a hand towel bounced next to them.

"Oh, is this where we're playing 7 minutes in heaven?"

Luc couldn't help it. He burst out laughing. Grabbing Cassie's hand, he ignored the blonde and headed out of the house with a giggling Cassie right beside him.

ABOUT THE AUTHOR

Rhian Cahill is the alter ego of a stay-at-home mother of four. With motherly duties rapidly dwindling, Rhian is able to make use of the fertile imagination she used to keep herself sane for all those years of slavery. Spending some years living overseas and visiting tropical climates has helped inspire some steamy stories. Multi-published in erotic romance and contemporary romance, Rhian, with the help of Mr. Muse, spends her days and nights writing.

When Rhian's not glued to the keyboard, you'll find her with book in hand, avoiding any and all housework as much as possible. For more on Rhian –

Website – http://www.rhiancahill.com/
Newsletter signup – http://eepurl.com/byrsf
Reader group - https://www.facebook.com/groups/211469429208895/
Twitter – https://twitter.com/RhianCahill
FaceBook – https://www.facebook.com/RhianCahillAuthor
Instagram – http://instagram.com/rhiancahill/
Goodreads page - https://www.goodreads.com/rhian_cahill

LOOK FOR THESE TITLES BY RHIAN CAHILL

Doing Logan
Bondi Beach Boys
Sand, Surf And Sunnie
Shut Up And Kiss Me
Christmas Wishes
New Year's Kisses
Valentine's Dates
Secret Santa
Secret Confessions: Sydney Housewives – Virginia
Secret Confessions: Backstage – Jet

Passport To Passion Collection
One Night In Bangkok
Singapore Fling

Coyote Hunger Series
Coyote Home – Book 1
Coyote Wild – Book 2
Coyote Whispers – Book 3

Look for these titles by Rhian Cahill

Only You Series
All Of You – Book 1

Party Games Series
Truth Or Dare
Spin The Bottle
Pass The Parcel – Novella

Are You Game Series
7 Minutes In Heaven – Book 1
Catch'n'Kiss – Book 2
Red Light, Green Light – Book 3

Frosty's Snowmen Series
A Touch Of Frost
A Kiss From Kringle
A Taste For Kandy

Hearts Are Wild Series
No More Talking (novella)
Dare You To (novella)
Mad Love

Dare To Love Kindle World Novellas
Her Daring Mistake
His Daring Moves

Sapphire Falls Kindle World Novella
Going Down Hard

Hope Falls Kindle World Novella
Love Me Like You Do

Wild Irish Kindle World Novella
Wild Rush

Look for these titles by Rhian Cahill

For a full list of Rhian's available books visit her website
http://www.rhiancahill.com/books/

CATCH'N'KISS EXCERPT

Have you read the other books in the *Are You Game?* series?

In the game of chase, a kiss is just an opening move

Divorced with two teenage daughters, party planner, Jody Walsh doesn't need any more complications in her life and her colleague Dan O'Conner is proving to be a big one.

It's not like one sensational stolen kiss is going to convince her to trust him with her heart, or her family, even if Dan's pursuit gives her bruised ego a desperately needed positive stroke.

It only took one kiss for Dan to know he wanted more with Jody, but the harder he chases, the more she runs. If only he could get her running in his direction.

When a night of passion doesn't convince Jody they're meant to be, Dan is left with no alternative but to prove he's worth the risk. He sets about demonstrating he can be trusted, but it's ultimately up to Jody to let her guard down and let him in.

This story features a heroine unwilling to risk her heart and a hero determine to persuade her why he's no risk at all.

Enjoy the following excerpt from Book 2 - *Catch'n'Kiss* –

Dan O'Conner reached for the warehouse door only for it to fly open and almost take his hand off. He took a half step back when a curvy behind appeared first through the doorway. Jody. She was bent at the waist, her lust inspiring curves on perfect display as she attempted to drag a huge box outside.

He stepped forward. "Here, let me help you."

"No, thanks. I've got it." She might not have snapped at him as usual, but there was a steel edge to Jody's voice that told him to back off.

"Whoa." Dan raised his hands and stepped out of the way as she cleared the doorway, tugging the box with her. Or trying to at least, but the thing was as wide as the door, and if she wasn't careful it would be wedged good and tight. "I was just offering to help."

Jody turned her head, flicking her blonde ponytail out, and lasered him with stormy-blue eyes. "And *I* said I've got it."

Dan took another step back. He had no clue why this woman didn't like him. It went beyond their initial introduction where he'd been pissed off at his boss, Cassie, for bringing in someone to share his workload. He'd been an ass about it all, and after that first day, Jody had avoided him or cut him off at the knees. The animosity hadn't improved one iota when he'd swallowed his pride and apologized for his behavior either. For some reason, Jody was still determined to dislike him. Which was a definite shame, because once he'd pulled his head out of his ass he'd realized she was one woman he wouldn't mind getting to know better.

Not that he'd take it beyond friendship even if she did like him. They worked together, and he'd been burned by a workplace relationship before. He wasn't about to tread in that territory again no matter how much his libido stood up and took notice whenever she was near. She wiggled her ass as she attempted to pull the huge box clear of the doorway, and Dan's pants got a little tighter. If she didn't want his help he'd be quite happy to stand here enjoying the view until he could sneak past and go inside.

A car pulled up behind him and Dan turned to see Cassie's

boyfriend—and Jody's brother—climb out of the driver's seat. "Hey, Luc."

Luc raised an eyebrow and tipped his chin in Jody's direction. "How's it going?"

"Good. You helping out tonight?" Dan asked.

"Nah, just a quick stop to see Cass before I have to get back to work." Luc stood beside Dan and eyed his sister. "Ah, Jody, do you want—"

"No!" Jody snapped as she yanked hard on the box. It sprang free of the frame and sent her stumbling back a couple of steps.

Dan and Luc both jumped out of the way to avoid a collision. Jeez, she really was in a mood. Good to see it wasn't just him she was lashing out at though. If she was that short with her brother, maybe it was her natural disposition and not anything to do with him. Except she was all smiles and laughs with everyone else at work most days. Stepping around the box, he grabbed the door. Jody huffed out a breath and stared at him. He could see her struggling to hold her tongue, so he smiled and pushed the door wider so it wasn't resting on the box and restricting its movement at all.

She narrowed her eyes and pulled her normally plush lips into a thin, straight line. "Don't you have things to do before we head out to the venue?"

Dan grinned. "Yeah, guess I do. See ya later, Luc." He wasn't stupid. He knew when he wasn't wanted, and if Jody was going to treat him like crap even the draw of checking out her hot bod couldn't convince him to hang around.

CPSIA information can be obtained
at www.ICGtesting.com
Printed in the USA
FSHW011943200819
61262FS

7 Minutes in Heaven

ARE YOU GAME?

7 Minutes is never enough

When you're building a business as the ultimate adult games party planner, you don't have time for games in real life but that's the problem Cassandra Moreland has when she butts heads with security expert Lucas Wilhelm.

Lucas is a six foot five wall of testosterone and a thorn in her side for wanting to shut her VIP party down early and she's not about to let him interfere without a fight, even if he is the first guy in a long time to get her heart racing and her palms sweating.

Lucas can't believe the pint-sized brunette is ready to go toe to toe with him. He's used to having his instructions obeyed without question, but Cassie has bigger balls than most guys he knows. The tightening in his groin and the pounding in his head has nothing to do with anger and everything to do with sexual interest.

The kind of interest that deserves a whole weekend of party games to explore.

This story features wet t-shirts, steamy sex and beads—but not the kind you think.

RHIAN CAHILL

www.rhiancahill.com

ISBN 978-1-925375-12-1